Clay Tagg＿＿＿＿＿＿＿＿＿ ＿＿＿ ＿＿ ＿＿＿ members of the band, a soldier s cap pulled low over his brow. It had been his idea to don the uniforms of slain troopers. He counted on the ruse fooling the Mexicans long enough to get in close to their camp, and in this he was proven right.

Slowing so that Delgadito and Cuchillo Negro could draw even with him, he said softly in their tongue, "I will take the smaller woman. Which one of you wants the other one?"

"We should just take the young one," Delgadito advised. "Later we can find more like her."

"Very well," Clay said, pulling ahead. "At my signal." His Winchester was balanced across his thighs. He gripped it and slowly pulled back the hammer so the click would not be loud. Then he let out with a bloodcurdling screech at the same instant he opened fire, levering off four shots so swiftly that two vaqueros were down and another wounded before the remainder awakened to their peril.

Delgadito and the rest took that action as their cue to cut loose, fanning out as they did. Their fierce war whoops were like the yipping of a frenzied pack of wolves.

The *White Apache* series published by
Leisure Books:
#1: HANGMAN'S KNOT
#2: WARPATH
#3: WARRIOR BORN
#4: QUICK KILLER

5

WHITE APACHE

BLOODBATH

Jake McMasters

LEISURE BOOKS   NEW YORK CITY

To Judy, Joshua, and Shane.

A LEISURE BOOK®

November 1994

Published by

Dorchester Publishing Co., Inc.
276 Fifth Avenue
New York, NY 10001

Printed in the United States of America.

Chapter One

The blazing sun scorched the dry earth of Sonora, Mexico.

Maria Gonzalez stared bleakly out the window of the carriage in which she rode. She was tired of the heat and dust. Most of all, she was upset because she was sweating so much.

Maria Gonzalez did not like to sweat. At the family hacienda she had servants who kept her cool every hour of every day. They bathed her when she was hot. They fanned her when she was the least bit uncomfortably warm. They brought her cool drinks when she was thirsty. The hacienda was heaven compared to the miserable carriage ride.

It bothered Maria that her father had decided to visit his brother at Janos. The family made the trip at least once a year, and it was a nightmare journey that Maria dreaded. The long hours on the dusty road, the constant jolting, the oppressive heat—all combined to make her utterly miserable. Small wonder that on these long journeys Maria missed the thousand and one little things her servants did for her throughout the day.

Maria Gonzalez never did anything for herself if she could have it done by others. She had been reared from infancy in the lap of luxury. Since she was old enough to walk, servants had waited on her every need and whim. They dressed her. They cooked her food and served it to her. They made her bed. They cleaned her room. They even saddled her horse when she wanted to go for an evening ride.

Yet here she was, many miles from the hacienda, without a single servant. On these trips she had to do everything for herself. Maria hated that. As one of the wealthiest senoritas in all of Mexico, she hated having to do menial work that was beneath her dignity. Why should she bathe herself? Why should she comb her own hair? Why should she have to fold her own clothes at night? It was an insult to her dignity.

The carraige suddenly hit a bump, throwing Maria into the air. She smoothed her dress, glared at the ribbon of road ahead, and then fixed her glare on her mother.

"Do not look at me like that, young lady," Theresa Gonzalez said stiffly. "I am not to blame for your suffering. If you must be mad at someone, be mad at your father."

"You let him bring me," Maria snapped. "I have every right to be as mad at you as I am at him."

"Why must we go through this every time we journey to Janos?" Theresa asked. "I should think

Bloodbath

that by now you would be used to this."

"I hate going and you know it," Maria said. "No matter how many times we make this trip I will never get used to it."

Theresa Gonzalez sniffed. "It saddens me that I have raised a daughter who can be so ungrateful. Your father loves you dearly. I would go so far as to say he spoils you. Yet once a year, when he asks you to make this little sacrifice, you always have one of your temper tantrums."

Maria opened her mouth to respond, but thought better of doing so. She might have said something that would have angered her mother. Then the stay at Janos would have been even worse. Her mother would have refused to speak to her. She would have been left alone with no one to talk to. Her father always forbade her to talk to the soldiers. Without her mother to talk to, she had no one.

Maria lowered her veil against the dust and stared out the window again. She had never been so depressed. She had to learn a way to prevent her father from forcing her to make these awful trips. After all, she was eighteen, a grown woman in her eyes and the eyes of many young men who came to court her.

At that exact moment, another pair of eyes were on Maria Gonzalez. Hidden behind a low bush so close to the road that he could have thrown a stone and hit the carriage was a Chiricahua Apache named Fiero. His bronzed body was covered with dirt that he had thrown over himself as camouflage. His face was pressed so close to the bush that they seemed to meld, which was exactly the impression Fiero wanted to give.

He had seen the carriage coming from a long way off. A plume of dust raised by its wheels and the hooves of the horses made the carriage easy to spot.

As Fiero watched the carriage go on by, his mind made note of several important facts. There were two men on top of the carriage—one driving and another armed with a rifle. Behind the carriage rode six men all well armed. In front of the carriage rode eight more men. And in front of them rode a tall bearded man who not only carried a rifle across his thighs, but also had three pistols strapped around his waist.

Fiero glanced again at the young woman he had caught a glimpse of. She was quite attractive for a *Nakai-yes*, not that Fiero had much interest in women. They were weaker than men, more emotional than men, and less skillful at war. Above all else, Fiero lived for war.

Fiero waited as motionless as a statue until the carriage and its escort were out of sight. Then he rose, and without bothering to brush himself clean, he turned and headed to the north at a trot that could eat up miles at a stretch. In his right hand he held a Winchester. On his right hip rode a big knife. His only clothing was a breechcloth. A red headband held his long black hair in place.

For half an hour Fiero ran. The hot sun beat without mercy on his broad back, but had no effect on him. His feet, covered by knee-high moccasins, slapped the hard ground in a steady cadence.

Presently Fiero came to rolling foothills. He

climbed swiftly using a deer trail. When he came to an arroyo he squated, cupped his hands to his mouth, and imitated the call of a red hawk. Moments later the strident cry was answered from deep within the arroyo.

Fiero descended the steep slope as nimbly as would a mountain sheep. At the bottom, where decades of erosion had worn a wide path, he ran fluidly, avoiding brush and boulders.

Not a Mexican alive knew that a small spring was located under a rock overhang where the arroyo merged with a hill. Here there were a few small trees, enough grass to graze a small number of horses for a week or so, and shade from the blistering heat.

As Fiero neared the spring he saw four fellow Apaches waiting for him. Or at least they looked like fellow Apaches, although in truth only three of them were.

Seated to the right of the spring was Delgadito. Formerly a warrior of repute, his standing in the Chiricahua tribe had fallen when he let his band be wiped out by savage scalphunters. For the longest while Delgadito had schemed to regain his lost esteem. But of late, he had not given the matter much thought. He had been content to roam far and wide raiding in Sonora, in Chihuahua, and along the border between Mexico and the United States. It pleased Delgadito immensely to bring suffering to those who had brought so much suffering to his people. It gave him a good feeling inside when he made the people of Sonora pay for having hired the scalphunters that had wiped out his band. It pleased him when he burned the wagons of white traders and tortured the traders

9

in return for the stealing of Apache lands by the white government.

Near Delgadito sat Chuchillo Negro. His name was Spanish for Black Knife. Amoung the Chiricahuas his skill with a knife was legendary. He could slit a man's throat in the blink of an eye. He was so quick that when he stabbed, his hands seemed to become invisible. Unlike Fiero, Chuchillo Negro did not kill for the sake of killing. Like Delgadito, he killed because he considered himself at war with both the whites and the *Nakai-yes* and he would continue on the warpath so long as blood pumped in his veins.

Kneeling at the water's edge was the youngest member of the band. His name was Ponce. His reason for killing was different from all the rest. Above all else Ponce wanted to be a great warrior. He aspired to become a leader of his tribe, a fighter whose fame would spread far and wide. Ponce had joined Delgadito's band to raid, kill, and plunder.

Most of Ponce's people were on a reservation, living in squalid poverty. It tore at the young warrior's insides to see them reduced to such a low state, and he hoped that one day he would lead them in an uprising to regain their ancient lands.

The fourth man at the spring was the one who was not an Apache. No one would have known it from his appearance. His hair was long and dark, like an Apache's. His skin had been burnt brown by the sun, like an Apache's. He wore a breechcloth, a headband, and moccasins, like an Apache. The one trait that marked him as a white man were his lake-blue eyes. And even they had a flinty aspect seldom seen in the eyes of whites.

This man had two names. In the white world he was known as Clay Taggart, a rancher who had gone bad. The Apaches knew him as Lickoyee-shis-inday.

Few whites knew it, but the Apaches had another name for themselves. They were the *Shis-Inday* in their own eyes—the men of the woods. So when Delgadito had named Clay Lickoyee-shis-inday, he had forever branded Taggart the white man of the woods.

For several months, the White Apache had roamed with his red brothers, going on raids deep into Mexico and attacking travelers north of the border. On this particular day, before Fiero arrived, Taggart had been gazing thoughtfully into the spring.

Clay Taggart marveled at the reflection that stared back at him. It amazed him that he was looking at the same man who only a year ago had been a typical Arizona rancher. If pressed, Clay would have been the first to admit that in his heart and soul he felt more Apache than white.

There had been a time when such thoughts would have troubled Taggart greatly. After all, for many years, he had considered Apaches the bane of the territory. That attitude was not uncommon—most whites hated the tribe. Whites wanted to see the Chiricahuas and other Apache branches wiped off the face of the earth. For Clay to have taken up with his lifelong enemies was a step so profound that even to this day he was sometimes bothered by it, but not for long.

Clay Taggart owed the Apaches a lot. He owed Degadito for saving his life. He owed the others for siding with him against his enemies. And above all else, Clay wanted vengeance on those who had wronged him.

Who could blame him? A wealthy rancher by the name of Miles Gillett had stolen Clay's land right out from under him. And worse, Gillett had stolen the woman whom Clay had loved.

Gillett had tried to have Clay killed. Had it not been for Delgadito's band, Clay would have been the guest of honor at a necktie social. Delgadito had saved Clay, taken him into his wickiup, and allowed his woman to nurse Clay back to health. Clay Taggart owed Delgadito a lot, and he was a man who believed in paying his debts.

In recent months, because of the many raids Clay had led, he had become the most wanted man in the territory. A 5,000 dollar bounty had been placed on his head, dead or alive, although it was no secret that most lawmen would have prefered the latter. Every sheriff and marshal north of the border and every law officer south of the border was on the lookout for him. Plus the U.S. Army was under standing orders to bring him in at all costs.

None of that concerned the White Apache overly much. So far he had eluded or slain all those who had been sent after him. Thanks to Delgadito and the others, his skills were so finely honed that only a true Apache could have hoped to have gotten close enough for a shot. And he was supremely confident that he could have eluded any who tried.

On this day, hearing Fiero mention the carriage and the young woman inside, the White Apache was reminded of an idea that had come to him

12

some time ago. He stared at each of the warriors in turn and then focused on Delgadito. "I say we capture this woman and take her with us."

Delgadito did not let his secret delight show. Lickoyee-shis-inday had shown no interest in women since being betrayed by the one he had loved. It was wonderful, though, Delgadito thought, that Taggart had finally seen the truth, which had sprouted from a seed of suggestion Delgadito had sown many days ago. But he had a part to play, so he said merely, "Why?"

"This one would be the first," White Apache said. "She and others like her are the key to our future."

"I do not follow the path of your words."

White Apache saw that he had everyone's attention and he stood. He chose his next words carefully, pronouncing them as best he was able. Since being saved by the band, he had toiled long and hard to learn their tongue. His effort had made him one of a handful of whites who spoke the Apache language fluently.

"I have been thinking, my brothers, about our situation," Clay said. "About how best we can pay the white-eyes back for the wrongs they have done us. We five have killed many or our enemies, taken much plunder, and punished those who have abused the Chiricahuas. But the five of us can only do so much. If our band were bigger, just think of how much more we could do. We would be able to go on twice as many raids, steal twice as many horses, kill twice as many of our enemies. The whites would tremble in fear."

Fiero snorted. "The Americans already fear us. In the settlements they talk of us in whispers.

They are afraid we will spring at them from out of nowhere if they say our names too loudly."

"What you say is true," Taggart said "but only to a point. The whites know there are only five of us. So while they fear us, they do not fear us as much as they would if there were ten or fifteen or even twenty of us." He gestured at each of them. "My kind have a saying: In numbers there is strength. What we need are more warriors."

Delgadito shifted and studied Taggart a few moments. "We know this as well as you, Lickoyee-shis-inday. We too would like to have more warriors join us. But no others are willing to leave the reservation because of what the soldiers would do to their families if they were caught." He folded his brawny arms. "I do not see how this one woman will draw them to us."

The White Apache squatted. "When you broke out of the reservation many moons ago, Delgadito, you had the right idea. You knew that for a band to survive, it must include women and children. Without their families, most warriors drift back to the reservation in time, no matter how opposed they are to the whites and the *Nakai-yes*. You were smart enough to take along the wives and children of all those who sided with you, insuring your band would stay intact and the warriors would never give up."

"I do not think that I was so smart. All the wives and children died." The reminder disturbed Delgadito greatly. Yes, once he had thought that he'd done the right thing, but he had changed his mind after the scalphunters had virtually wiped out his band. War was for warriors, Fiero often said, and Delgadito had come to think the firebrand was right. Women and children had to stay on the reservation where they were safe.

Clay Taggart went on. "If we are to see this band grow, we must show the warriors on the reservation that we are strong enough to withstand the whites and the Mexicans at every turn. We must build their confidence in us. And there is no better way to do that than to have women and children of our own. Once the reservation warriors see that we have families, they will feel free to bring their own and join us."

Fiero saw that his companions were moved by the idea, and he quickly spoke against it. "Women and children are not so easy to come by. They do not sprout from the soil like plants."

"True," Clay said, "but there are plenty out there for the taking—like this woman you saw. Each of us will steal a wife and a child or two, and in no time we will be a true band of Apaches. Your brothers on the reservation will no longer see us as isolated warriors fighting a lost cause."

It was Cuchillo Negro who spoke next. "Your words ring true, Lickoyee-shis-inday. But they are not practical. You were with us when Blue Cap and his men wiped out our families and friends. You saw the slaughter. How can you ask us to risk the same thing all over again?"

"Look at it this way," Clay answered. "You are at war with the white-eyes who took your land from you and forced all of your people onto the reservation. To win your war, you must take risks." He paused. "I happen to be at war with those who stole my land out from under me and tried to stretch my neck. And I would risk anything, *do* anything, to see they get what is coming to them." He paused again. "How about all of you? How badly do you want to see the white-eyes pay?"

Clay did not wait for an answer. He knew that if he did, a few of them might elect to argue the point. When dealing with Apaches, he had learned it was better to seize the bull by the horns, as it were. Rising, he strode off down the arroyo, saying over a shoulder, "I will go to see if this woman is worth taking. Any who wants to come can."

Rare hesitation gripped the warriors. Fiero was the first to follow in the White Apache's steps, but not because he wanted to waste time stealing women. He simply couldn't resist a chance to spill more blood, and there promised to be plenty spilled if Lickoyee-shis-inday tried to wrest the senorita from her protectors.

Ponce was the next to stand. In order for him to earn the reputation of a great war chief, he must never shirk a chance to go into battle. The thought of stealing women mattered little to him. Not very long ago he had lost the woman he wanted as his wife to an army scout sent to kill the band, and he had not yet recovered from her loss.

Cuchillo Negro and Delgadito stood together and walked from the spring side by side. Cuchillo Negro glanced at the former leader and let the corners of his mouth prick upward.

"He plays right into your hands, does he not?"

"Into our hands, you mean."

"I am not the one who craves to be a leader again. I am not the one who needs to build up a large band to see his fondest wish come true."

"Do you hold it against me?"

Bloodbath

"No," Cuchillo Negro said. "What is good for you is good for all our people, and what is good for us is good for Lickoyee-shis-inday. The more of us there are, the easier it will be for him to take his revenge on those who wronged him."

"I still do not understand why you like him so."

Cuchillo Negro stared at the rippling muscles on the white man's back. "I am proud to call him my friend. He has put his life in danger many times to save ours. What more need he do to prove his worth to you?"

"He is white. Never forget that."

"His skin was white once. Deep inside, I suspect, he has always been Apache and just not known it."

Further talk was brought to an end by Clay Taggart, who broke into a trot, forcing the rest to do the same to keep up. Clay intended to reach a certain spot bordering the road to Janos before the carriage passed by, which meant they must hurry.

The White Apache felt the warmth of the sun on his shoulders and the dry wind caress his face. The land around him gave off shimmering waves of heat. Once he would have withered in that burning inferno like a pampered houseplant suddenly thrust outdoors. Now he savored the sensation.

Clay Taggart knew he was a man reborn. The Apache way of life had forged his body into a vibrant whipcord of power and speed. He was three times the man he had been before he'd joined Delgadito, and he reveled in the change.

The time passed swiftly. From atop the last of

17

the foothills the White Apache spied the pale track of the road. He made for a cluster of boulders adjacent to it. Once there, he checked both ways before stepping to the middle of the rutted track to see if the carriage had already gone by. To his annoyance, it had, not more than half an hour before, judging by a pile of fresh horse droppings.

"We are too late," he said.

When Fiero grunted and pointed northward, the White Apache looked. His eyes were not anywhere near as sharp as Fiero's but they were sharp enough to spot the distant riders coming toward them—riders who wore the uniforms of Mexican soldiers.

Chapter Two

Capt. Vincente Filisola had always had a weakness for the ladies. Ever since the age of seven, when he accidentally caught sight of a cousin taking a bath, he had been keenly fascinated by the female form.

Being the dashing man that Filisola was, he had more than his fair share of conquests to boast of—which he never did since he was a perfect gentleman. But he often thought about them. Even when on duty, in the midst of the desert, Filisola would let his mind drift, savoring each delicious memory.

Of late, though, the poor captain had few such conquests to reminisce about. Being posted to the frontier had turned out to be a calamity for a very simple reason: there were too few women to satisfy his constant craving.

In Mexico City it had been different. Filisola could have dated a different senorita every night.

Janos was another story altogether. A small, pathetic town that probably would have dried up and blown away if not for the garrison there, it could boast of few attractive prospects. Most of the women were plump matrons, as appealing to the captain as roast pork, which he detested. The score or so of unmarried women were either desperate spinsters or untouched maidens kept under lock and key by wisely protective fathers.

It was so distressing a situation that Capt. Filisola had taken to running up quite a tab at the cantina he frequented. The alcohol helped to drown his sorrow at the cruel fate that had befallen him. His tour at Janos had become one of abject despair.

And then Filisola saw her. Not half an hour earlier the captain had been surprised to come upon a carriage under armed escort. He had reined up as the party approached, slapped some of the dust from his uniform, and put on his most officious air.

The man leading the party had an air that was more commanding than the captain's. He drew rein and, without bothering to introduce himself, asked, "How is the road between here and the post?"

Capt. Filisola had half a mind to tell the rude stranger that he could ride on and find out for himself. But he held his tongue. Having to deal with temperamental superior officers on a regular basis had bred a certain degree of tact in him, which served him in good stead.

"We saw no sign of savages, senor," he answered. "I would advise you to proceed with caution anyway. There have been reports of Apache raids near Hermosillo."

The bearded man adjusted his sombrero. "How well I know the dangers," he said, half to himself. "We make this trip once a year. I am Martin Gonzalez, by the way."

"Gonzalez?" Filisola repeated. "Are you any relation to Col. Jose Gonzalez, the officer in charge at Janos?"

"He is my brother."

Vicente Filisola inwardly thanked the Madonna that he had not given his tongue free rein. Stiffening, he gave a little bow and introduced himself, adding, "I would be remiss in my duty if I did not put my men and myself completely at your service. If you want, we will go with you the rest of the way to guarantee your safe passage."

Filisola had an ulterior motive. He despised long patrols. If Martin Gonzalez agreed, he could cut this one short and return to Janos. In two days he would be in the cantina drowning his sorrows again. At least it was cool there.

Just then a figure appeared in the carriage window. The captain's pulse quickened as a veil was lifted to reveal a beautiful young woman, the likes of whom he had not seen since leaving Mexico City six months earlier. His breath caught in his throat. Something on Filisola's face made Martin Gonzalez turn.

"Ah. This is my daughter Maria, Captain."

"I am honored, senorita," Filisola said with all the dignity he could muster.

Maria grinned, showing teeth as white as pearls. "My, my. You must be new to the post. I know I would remember if I had met so dashing an officer on my last visit."

21

Martin Gonzalez lifted his reins. "I am sorry to cut this short, but we have many more miles to cover before sunset. Since we will be at Janos for a week or two, perhaps you will do us the honor of coming to supper one evening? That is, if your duties will permit it."

Maria's smile widened. "Oh, please do. I starve for polite conversation when I am there."

"I would be honored," Filisola said, bowing again. When Filisola straightened up, Gonzalez was already in motion. He doffed his cap to the daughter, who gave him the sort of inviting look that brought gooseflesh to his skin.

Only when the Gonzalez party had dwindled to the size of ants did Filisola ride on. So euphoric was he over the chance encounter that he had gone a quarter of a mile before he realized with a start that he would be unable to see Maria again. He was under orders to patrol far to the south and west of Hermosillo, a task that would take him the better part of three weeks. By the time he returned to Janos, Maria Gonzalez would be gone.

That thought put the captain in a foul mood. After so much time he had finally met someone who ignited his passion, yet he would be unable to have the pleasure of her company! Sometimes life could be so unfair it hurt.

Caught up in his inner turmoil, the young officer failed to pay much attention to his surroundings or to give any thought to the Apaches reputed to be in the region. He spied a large cluster of boulders bordering the road, but he did not give them a second thought.

All he could think of was Maria Gonzalez.

Bloodbath

*   *   *

Hidden among those boulders, the White Apache firmed his grip on his Winchester and allowed himself a grim smile. Few of the weary soldiers showed any interest in their surroundings, an often fatal mistake in the wilderness. Even the officer had his eyes on the road. They were riding right into the ambush.

White Apache glanced to the right, where Fiero was concealed, and then to the left, where Cuchillo Negro had gone to ground. Neither were visible. Nor were Delgadito or Ponce, who were across the road. The soldiers would never know what had hit them.

Clay placed his cheek flat on the ground and listened to the approaching drum of hoofbeats. Soon he heard the creak of saddles, the rattle of accoutrements and the nicker of horses. A soldier coughed.

It was up to Clay to give the signal. He waited until he judged that fully half of the patrol had gone past his position; then he surged to his knees and uttered a piercing Apache war whoop. At the same time he jammed the rifle stock to his shoulder and fired at the nearest trooper. In that instant, all hell broke loose.

Delgadito, Cuchillo Negro, Fiero, and Ponce also popped up and cut loose, their rifles decimating the patrol in the span of seconds. Men and horses went down, some of the men cursing and screaming, some of the animals squealing in agony.

The first soldier Clay shot had the side of his head blown off. Clay pivoted, aimed at a second Mexican, and sent a slug into the man's chest. As

23

he took aim at a third, another throaty war whoop rose above the general din and Fiero hurtled from out among the boulders, a glistening knife in his right hand.

Like a diving bird of prey, Fiero swooped down onto a mounted soldier, landing astride the horse behind his quarry. The soldier tried to bring his carbine into play. Fiero merely gripped the man's hair, yanked the head back, and slit the man's throat with a neat, swift stroke.

Ponce had also charged into the fray, shooting his rifle as fast as targets presented themselves.

The patrol broke and scattered, few of the soldiers having the nerve to stand and fight. But there was one exception.

Clay had risen for a better shot at a fleeing trooper when out of the corner of one eye he glimpsed the young officer. The man had courage. A pistol in hand, the brash captain was bearing down on Ponce, who was too busy shooting to notice. Clay spun, took a hasty bead, and stroked the trigger.

At the blast, the officer jerked backward, but somehow was able to cling to his saddle horn. Doubled over, swaying badly, the man hauled on the reins, cutting to the right to swing wide of the boulders. In moments his mount was in full flight off across the desert.

The White Apache aimed deliberately. He was on the verge of firing when a bullet spanged off the boulder in front of him. It sent rock slivers into his cheek. Whirling, he discovered a wounded soldier in the middle of the road reloading to fire again. Clay cored the man's head from front to back.

Bloodbath

Suddenly the gunfire died out. Eleven soldiers lay dead or dying in the dust. Five horses were down, five more milled about in confusion. The eleventh had raced off in a panic.

Fiero, with feral glee, was dispatching the wounded. Ponce stood ready, covering him. Only Delgadito and Cuchillo Negro remembered Clay's instructions and dashed out to claim the loose mounts.

The White Apache ran to a fine sorrel and grasped its bridle. The horse shied at his unfamiliar scent. It tried to pull free but Clay hung on and spoke softly to soothe the animal's fears. After it quieted down, he looped the reins around a dry bush.

A gravely wounded soldier, no more than 18 years old by the looks of him, had been propped against a boulder. Fiero had ripped off the trooper's shirt and was carving off thin strips of flesh. Delgadito and Cuchillo Negro had caught three horses. Ponce, seeing them, nabbed a fourth.

Clay reached Fiero as the warrior lowered his knife to inflict more suffering. The hapless soldier, too weak to cry out, could only watch with dazed eyes as the bloody blade bit into his skin.

"We have no time for this," White Apache said. "I told you what was most important and you did not listen."

The firebrand looked up, his hand poised on the knife. "You forget yourself, Lickoyee-shis-inday. White-eyes and *Nakai-yes* take orders from others, but never Apaches. We are free to do as we want, when we want. We only do as our leaders say when it suits us."

There had been a time when Clay would have

25

flown off the handle at such a reply. The band had, after all, picked him as leader over his strong objections, so it was only fair that the warriors do as he wanted. But Apaches were notoriously independent. Every man was his own master. No warrior did anything he did not want to do. For Clay to criticize the Apache way would only sour Fiero against him, and he needed the fiery troublemaker as much as he needed the others.

"For the plan to work," Clay said, "we must all do our part. Am I to take it that you do not want to join us this time?"

"I never said that," Fiero snapped. With a sharp flick of his thick wrist he drove the razor-sharp blade into the young soldier's heart. The man gurgled once and perished. "I will help you even though I think it foolish to burden ourselves with women and children."

Delgadito came over, carrying a shirt he had stripped from a slain soldier. "I hope you know what you are doing," he said in heavily accented English. He liked to speak the strange, birdlike language as often as he could just to keep in practice. After having labored so hard to learn it while teaching Taggart the Apache tongue, he did not care to let his newfound ability go to waste.

Clay gave the warrior a friendly clap on the shoulder. "You and me both, pard," he said. "If I don't, they're liable to put windows in our skulls before we get off a shot."

Capt. Filisola became aware of low voices and of fingers probing his temple. Thinking he had fallen into the clutches of the dreaded Apaches, he automatically grabbed the hand and sat bolt upright. The abrupt movement lanced his skull with pain. Pinwheeling points of light danced before his eyes. It was several moments before his vision cleared and he saw that he held Sgt. Amat.

"Can you stand, captain? Or would you like help?"

Filisola realized eight other troopers stood around him. "I can manage." He blinked a few times, girded his legs, and rose unsteadily. There was a nasty gash on his temple and he had lost a lot of blood, but he would live. "Did those red devils get all the rest?"

"I don't know. I have not been back to check." Sgt. Amat gestured at the barren expanse of desert. "I have been busy rounding up this bunch. If I had not spotted your horse, we would never have found you."

The bay stood nearby, caked with sweat. Filisola turned and was surprised to find the road no longer in sight. "How far did it carry me?" he asked.

"About two miles," Amat said. "I would guess you have been unconscious for an hour and a half."

"That long?" Filisola said, appalled. In that amount of time the Apaches could have done as they pleased with any of his men they took alive. "Mount up. Pronto. We must go see."

"Yes, Captain."

Their reluctance was obvious, and Filisola couldn't blame them. For more years than anyone could remember, Apaches had been raiding the states of Sonora and Chihuahua, striking at will. Countless men had been massacred, women and children carried away, whole districts laid to waste. Small wonder, then, that most who lived in northern Mexico regarded Apaches as demons incarnate rather than mere mortals.

Filisola didn't share that belief, thanks to an incident that had taken place six years earlier. He had been a lieutenant then, assigned to the staff of a general. The general had been making the rounds of remote outposts when the column stopped for the night at an isolated spring.

Filisola had been asleep during the night when a sentry sounded an alarm. Leaping to his feet, Filisola had dashed toward the horse string, where a tremendous commotion had been taking place. In the dark he had nearly bumped into another running figure. He had assumed it was a fellow soldier until a stray gleam from the flickering fire revealed a young Apache who had been caught in the act of trying to steal a few horses.

They had set eyes on one another at the same instant. Filisola had his pistol in hand. The stripling had a knife, nothing more. In sheer reflex Filisola had fired, and his slug had ripped through the Apache's stomach, dropping the warrior where he stood. It was then, as Filisola watched blood spurt from the lethal wound and saw the acute pain reflected on the warrior's face, that he had realized Apaches were flesh-and-blood creatures like himself, not inhuman monsters.

The memory comforted Filisola as he trotted toward the road. He wished he had some way of imparting the knowledge to those under him since it was apparent they would bolt if set upon again.

Bloodbath

Moments later Amat called out and jabbed a finger at the sky. Filisola titled his head and placed a hand across his eyebrows to shield his eyes from the harsh glare. The stark silhouettes of ungainly big birds flew in circles on the horizon.

"Already!" Filisola barked in disgust.

"The buzzards must eat when they can," Amat said.

Jabbing his mount in the flanks, Filisola brought his horse to a gallop. The soldiers did the same, riding in a short column of twos, their carbines at the ready.

The captain slowed down when the boulders were less than 500 yards off. He divided his small command in half and sent the sergeant to the left while he went to the right. Boulders hid the grisly tableau until he came to the edge of the road.

Vultures were everywhere—on the bodies of the men, on the few dead horses, and on the boulders. The birds were waiting to feed. The rank odor of blood hung heavy in the hot air, as did another foul odor that made Filisola want to retch. He held the urge in check and dismounted.

"Mother of God!" one of the troopers said.

So much blood had been spilled that a sticky layer caked the road. A number of the slain had been mutilated. A few had had their throats slit wide. One soldier had been gutted, then strangled to death with his own intestines. Even one of the mounts had been carved up, which was not unusual. It was widely known that Apaches ate horseflesh.

Filisola held his breath and advanced. A vulture hissed at him, but gave way when Filisola took another stride. With its huge wings flapping loudly, the bird slowly climbed into the air and soared off. Others did likewise. A few refused to budge even though Filisola shouted at them and waved his arms.

One particular vulture saw fit to peck out the eyeball of a dead trooper. It paused to glare at the officer, the eyeball dangling from its beak by a thread. Racked by revulsion, Filisola shot the bird dead. At the sound of the gunshot the rest flew off. Filisola looked up to see over 20 circling high overhead, biding their time.

"Bastards," he growled under his breath.

Sgt. Amat came from the other direction. Halting, he covered his nose and mouth. "All the men are now accounted for, Captain."

"Yes," Filisola said sadly. He knew that his superior, Col. Gonzales, would be furious with him. It wouldn't surprise him if the colonel called a board of inquiry to determine if he had been negligent.

"Strange, is it not, sir?" the sergeant said.

"What is?" Filisola asked absently.

"Apaches usually don't bother to take clothes. Why do you suppose they did this time?"

Only then did it occur to Filisola that a number of the bodies lacked shirts and pants. And some, he was puzzled to note, had been stripped of their boots.

A half-breed had once revealed to Filisola that Apaches had a deep dread of the dead. The half-breed had claimed that after a raid, Apaches went through a purification ceremony. Furthermore, Apaches were reputed to burn any article that touched a dead person in the belief that the

Bloodbath

article would bring nothing but bad medicine. Why then, the officer wondered, had this band made an exception to the general rule?

"Should we bury them?" Amat inquired.

"Need you ask?"

"No, sir." Amat pivoted and issued commands. A burial detail was hastily formed and the men set to work digging.

Filisola moved to a small boulder and sat down. He had a decision to make. Should he continue on his patrol or report the clash to the colonel? With so few men he stood little chance of catching the band. He might as well go back, he reflected.

There was another factor Filisola had to consider. If the band responsible for the Hermosillo raids had been the same one that sprang the ambush, it was safe to assume they were heading in the same direction as the Gonzalez family, which put the family in great peril. It was his responsibility to warn them.

The officer decided to head back just as soon as the last corpse was laid to rest. He idly scanned the grisly unfortunates. Six of them were without shirts, five without pants, five without boots. His gaze roved and he spied a torn shirt across the road. That made the numbers even. Five complete uniforms had been taken.

"Why only five?" he mused aloud. Had there only been five Apaches? It had seemed as if there were many more.

Seconds later the sergeant hurried up. "Captain, five horses are still unaccounted for. They must have run off. Say the word, and I will take a private and go hunt for them."

"Five horses?" Filisola said, troubled by the

news although he could not say why. Apaches stole horses all the time. So what if they had stolen some now? But then he thought of the five uniforms.

"Yes," Amat said. "What would you have us do?"

Instead of responding, Filisola rose and walked to the north. He was not much of a tracker but he tried to read the prints anyway. Between the boulders it was impossible. There were too many jumbled together. Past the boulders he came on a spot at the side of the road where he found moccasin prints, bare footprints, and boot tracks. It took him a minute to appreciate the significance.

"Dear God," Filisola said.

"Captain?" Amat said. "I do not understand? What is the matter?"

Filisola had to be sure. He ran a dozen yards farther. The tracks made by the five horses were easy to make out, all bearing to the northeast. The ravishing image of Maria Gonzalez filled his mind, and he shuddered as if cold. "Forget the graves. We must mount and ride."

"But we owe it to those who were slain to give them a decent burial," Amat objected.

"Our first duty is to the living, not the dead," Capt. Filisola said. "Now get the men on their horses, or you will be the one who will explain to our colonel why we did not arrive in time to save his brother from the Apaches."

Sgt. Amat glanced at the ground, then at the winding road. The color drained from his face and he spun on a heel. Snarling orders, he had the men on their mounts in record time.

To Capt. Vicente Filisola, it wasn't fast enough.

Chapter Three

Adobe Wells had been aptly named. It was located on the road that led from Hermosillo to Janos. The village was a day-and-a-half ride from the border between the states of Sonora and Chihuahua. An old well was the chief attraction. Nearby were the ruins of an adobe house. Countless weary travelers had stopped there over the years. This night, it was the Gonzalez party.

The cool of the evening brought refreshing relief to Maria Gonzalez. She donned her silk wrap and went for a short stroll to stretch her legs. The pair of vigilant vaqueros her father had told to tag along stayed a discreet distance behind to afford her privacy.

Maria made a slow circuit of the ruins, often turning her face into the invigorating breeze. She would have given anything for a long soak in a tub or to have a servant fan her while she sipped a cold drink. It was unthinkable that such luxuries were to be denied her until she returned to the hacienda.

Maria toyed with the idea of having a vaquero fan her, but did not because she knew her father would not approve. She walked toward the well, pausing when the distant wail of a lonely coyote rent the tranquil desert. She felt sympathy for that coyote, which she imagined to be all alone in the middle of nowhere, just as she was. Then she heard another wail and another, and she knew the coyote was with others of its kind.

The thought reminded Maria of the handsome captain. How sad, she mused, that she was denied the pleasure of his company. His gracious manner had marked him as a true gentleman, just the sort of man whose company she preferred. She craved a few hours of witty talk and merry laughter almost as much as she did a bath.

There were footsteps behind her. Maria turned and inwardly steeled herself. The look on her mother's face warned her that she was in trouble again. She put on a bold front, saying sweetly, "Have you come for a drink, mother?"

"I have come to talk, daughter," Theresa Gonzalez said sternly. "Your father is very upset with you and wants me to set you straight."

"What have I done this time?" Maria said, thinking that her father's anger must have something to do with her complaints about the trip and the barbaric conditions she was forced to endure.

"I think you know. Your father says that you were brazenly flirting with that young officer this afternoon."

"Nonsense. All I did was exchange pleasantries," Maria said, genuinely surprised. "Where did father ever get such a crazy notion? How could I have flirted when I was seated in the carriage?"

"Do not play the offended innocent with me," Theresa said. "I did my share of flirting before I wed your father. I know that all a woman has to do is bat her eyes a certain way and it is the same as exposing herself."

"Mother!" Maria said, shocked as much by the admission as the crude comparison.

"Don't look at me like that. Do you think I am a saint? All young women flaunt their charms. It is the bait with which we hook the fish of our dreams." Despite herself, Maria broke into gay laughter. "Even so, I was being no more than polite to Capt. Filisola. As a general rule I do not flirt with a man unless I have known him at least five minutes."

Now it was the mother's turn to laugh. "I was the same at your age." She clasped her hands to her bosom. "Oh, Maria, how I envy you. Savor this time. These years are some of the most wonderful you will ever know."

"Married life will be wonderful too."

"Oh, it will be, but in a different way. Once a woman takes a man into her life, everything changes. She has new responsibilities, new burdens. Nothing is ever the same again."

That last comment was uttered almost wistfully, prompting Maria to ask, "Do you regret marrying father?"

"Certainly not. As men go, he is better than most. He doesn't beat me or drink to excess. And he works hard, that man, so very hard. Sometimes I think his work will be the death of him. It is all

I can do to get him to take time off once a year for this trip."

Insight made Maria gasp. "So that is why you refuse to put a stop to these nightmare journeys?"

"Stop them? Child, I encourage them. As you will no doubt learn, men are stubborn creatures. Their pride makes them believe they are invincible. Your father knows he must take time off, but he never would if not for me." Theresa gave a wise smile. "Women must always use their wiles when dealing with men. Managing a husband is a lot like managing an oversize ten year old."

Maria politely placed a hand over her mouth to stifle an unladylike snort. It was rare that her mother talked so frankly with her, and she enjoyed it immensely. "Tell me more," she said.

Theresa hooked her arm around her daughter's and strolled back toward the fire. "Another time, perhaps. Supper is almost ready."

One of the vaqueros had made the meal—a tangy rabbit stew flavored by the roots of a plant the vaquero had picked along the route.

Maria ate hers slowly, glad the vaquero was along so she did not have to soil her hands cooking. It had never failed to amaze her how self-sufficient the vaqueros were. They prepared their own food when they were away from the ranch, mended their own clothes when necessary, and took care of their own horses. All the little things that servants did for her, they did themselves. Secretly, she pitied them and frequently gave thanks that she had not been born poor.

Suddenly a burly vaquero with a jagged scar on his right cheek hastened out of the darkness to her father's side. "Pardon, sir. Riders come."

Martin Gonzalez rose, his brow furrowed. "Who could it be at this hour, Pedro? Fellow travelers perhaps?"

"Maybe," Pedro said. He had worked for the Gonzalez family for over 20 years and was as loyal to the brand as any Texas cowpuncher would have been. "But to be safe, perhaps you should take the senora and the senorita and go in among the ruins."

"You would have us hide, Pedro?" Martin responded. "What would my men think of me if they saw me act like a coward?"

"They know that you have your family to think of," Pedro said, refusing to be cowed. All that mattered to him was the safety of those he worked for.

The other vaqueros had gathered around, some with rifles, others with their hands resting on their pistols. All of them heard the beat of hooves, the creak of leather, and the clank of gear, such as a cavalry patrol might make.

"It must be the officer we met today," Martin Gonzalez said and glanced sharply at his daughter. "I wonder what prompted him to turn back to Janos."

"Don't look at me," Maria said, a trifle indignant. "All I did was pass the time of the day with the man."

Many of the vaqueros had started to relax. A few had turned to go about their business.

Martin cupped his hands to his mouth. "Is that you, Capt. Filisola?" he called.

"Yes," came the muted reply.

"There. You see?" Martin said to Pedro. "As I

thought, we have nothing to worry about. Put on another pot of coffee for our guests. They have been on the trail all day and will be grateful for our hospitality."

Maria set down her bowl and stood. She needed several minutes to freshen herself so she would look her best for the dashing captain. Without saying a word to her parents, she slipped off toward the ruins, grinning at the thought of the pleasant interlude she was about to have.

But she was wrong.

The White Apache rode in front of the other members of the band, a soldier's cap pulled low over his brow. It had been his idea to don the uniforms of slain troopers. He counted on the ruse fooling the Mexicans long enough to get in close to their camp, and in this he was proven right.

Clay answered the hail, his hand over his mouth to muffle his voice. He saw vaqueros clustered near the fire. There were also two women present, not one. Slowing so that Delgadito and Cuchillo Negro could draw even with him, he said softly in their tongue, "I will take the smaller woman. Which one of you wants the other one?"

"Not me," Cuchillo Negro said. "Look at her. She has many winters behind her, and old *Nakai-yes* make poor wives. They do not hold up well."

"We should just take the young one," Delgadito advised. "Later we can find more like her."

"Very well," Clay said, pulling ahead. "At my signal." His Winchester was balanced across his thighs. He gripped it and slowly pulled back the hammer so the click would not be loud.

The younger woman had risen and was moving toward the ruins. A bearded man was giving directions to a swarthy vaquero.

Martin Gonzalez saw several silhouettes materialize in the gloom. The foremost rider wore a trooper's cap, he could tell. Martin took a step to greet the newcomers when it occurred to him that the hat was the kind worn by privates, not the shorter version worn by officers. It was strange, he thought, that a private would be out in front of the patrol. By tradition, officers usually assumed the lead.

Clay noticed the bearded man staring hard at him. He suspected the man was suspicious, and not wanting to lose the element of surprise, he let out with a bloodcurdling screech at the same instant he opened fire, levering off four shots so swiftly that two vaqueros were down and another wounded before the remainder awakened to their peril.

Delgadito and the rest took that action as their cue to cut loose, fanning out as they did. Their fierce war whoops were like the yipping of a frenzied pack of wolves.

To say the vaqueros were taken unawares would be an understatement. Pedro was the first of the stunned group to overcome the daze that gripped him. Frantically, he clawed at his pistol. Others did likewise, but Taggart and the Apaches ducked low and weaved, proving difficult targets to hit.

Theresa Gonzalez screamed, a hand to her throat. She was too terrified by the sight of one of the riders bearing down on her to move.

Vaguely she realized her husband had sprung to her aid and felt his arm encircle her waist. As she fell to the ground, she twisted and saw the Indian veer aside.

Maria Gonzalez was terrified. Her feet were rooted to the ground. A thick cloud of choking gunsmoke clogged the air, and bullets whizzed by her to the left and right. As a rider bore down on her, she glimpsed his raven shock of black hair and felt raw fear knife through her insides. It galvanized her into racing for the ruins.

All of her life Maria had heard stories about Apaches—awful tales of the atrocities they committed, of the many women and children who had been abducted. Her own cousin, a sweet girl of 16, had been taken several years ago. Eventually the girl's father had been able to bargain for her release. The whole family had turned out to welcome her and been shocked beyond measure when it became apparent the girl's mind was gone.

The mere thought of suffering the same horrid fate was enough to make Maria dizzy with fear. She gritted her teeth and willed her legs to pump. Directly ahead appeared a low adobe wall. She was confident she would be safe once she hid behind it.

The drum of hooves grew louder and louder, becoming thunder in her ears. Maria was almost to the ruins when she glanced over her left shoulder and saw the rider right behind her. "No!" she cried, darting to the left to escape.

The White Apache anticipated such a move. He leaned far out, his left arm held low, and caught the fleeing female about her slim waist.

Pulling upward with all his might, he swung her up in front of him. She seemed to weigh next to nothing.

"No!" Maria wailed. "Father! Mother! Help me!" She kicked and tried to hit her captor, but it was as if she struck solid rock.

Over by the fire, Martin and Theresa Gonzalez heard the terrified shriek of their offspring. Both forgot their own safety and rushed to her rescue, Martin with a pistol in each hand. They spotted a horse bearing two figures and knew it had to be an Apache making off into the night with their pride and joy.

"Save our child!" Theresa screamed.

Martin tried. He aimed carefully, but had to hold his fire when the mount swerved just as he was about to squeeze the trigger. In the dark he couldn't be sure if he would hit the warrior or Maria.

"Shoot! Shoot!" Theresa said.

Again Martin took aim, but by this time the figures were shrouded by the night. "I can't!" he replied. "I might kill her by accident!"

Racked by despair, the desperate parents watched the Apache vanish into the desert. Martin whirled. Of the 17 men he had brought along, eight were down. "Anyone who can, follow me!" he roared. "Those bastards have stolen my daughter!"

Martin sprinted toward the horse string, only to discover the horses were gone. Drawing up short, he glared at the empty space where the animals had been. "This can't be!" he raged.

From out of murk rushed Pedro, blood trickling from a cleft cheek, where he had been nicked by a slug. "Two of those devils drove the horses off! Do not worry, sir. We will find them and save Maria."

Martin could only nod dumbly as several vaqueros dashed into the darkness to retrieve the animals. He knew how fast Apaches could travel. By the time the horses were rounded up, the band would be many miles away. The odds of rescuing Maria were slender, at best.

Clenching his fists in impotent fury, Martin threw back his head to rail at the wind, then changed his mind. He must be strong, if only for his wife's sake. Theresa was a kind, sensitive soul and the very best of wives, but she did not handle a crisis well. He recalled how once, when a relative of theirs had been kidnapped by Apaches, she had stayed in their room for days, weeping constantly. If she believed Maria was lost to them forever, there was no telling what she might do.

Martin Gonzalez turned to go comfort his wife. He wished that he'd had the good sense to ask that young captain to accompany them to the fort. His brother would have understood.

Pausing, Martin listened, hoping to hear the sound of the Apache mounts in the distance. All he heard, though, were the shouts of his vaqueros and the sighing of the wind.

Oh, Maria! he thought. My poor baby!

Maria Gonzalez ceased to struggle after a while. The Apache was too strong for her. And she did not care to make him mad. Apaches were masters at torture.

Many years ago Maria had seen the body of a lone traveler waylaid by Mescalero Apaches; they had gouged out his eyes, cut off his nose and ears, removed his tongue, and whittled him down until he was more bone than flesh. She would never forget that sight as long as she lived.

Behind her, the White Apache was pleased by the fact the captive no longer fought back. He had expected her to tear into him tooth and nail or to go into hysterics. Her composure impressed him. He assumed she must have great courage, which would serve her well in the days and weeks to come.

What Taggart had not expected, however, was the strange sensation that came over him at being so close to a woman after having been denied female companionship for so long. The soft feel of her body against his, the perfumed scent of her luxurious hair, and the earthy scent of her skin were enough to arouse stirrings in him the likes of which he had not felt since he had lost the woman he loved to Miles Gillett.

It disturbed Clay Taggart that he should feel this way. Of late he had taken inordinate pride in the degree of self-control he now had over his mind and body. He flattered himself that he sometimes exercised the same masterful discipline as the Chiricahuas. But clearly that was not the case.

Taggart shifted in the saddle to give the woman a little more room. He checked and verified that all five warriors trailed him. There was no sign of pursuit yet. It wouldn't be long before the woman's kin and the vaqueros came after them.

Long into the night Taggart and his band pressed on. They rode their horses to near exhaustion, stopping only when a pink band framed the eastern skyline.

In the foothills of the Sierra Madre Mountains, Taggart finally stopped. He slid off and, without thinking, offered his hand to the woman, who alighted as if stepping barefoot onto crushed glass.

Maria studied her captor, trying her best to conceal her fright. She noted his hard, cruel features, and the rippling muscles of his arms and stomach. He was studying her in turn. Maria looked into his eyes and was amazed to see they were blue.

Taggart could not help but notice the woman's reaction. It wasn't hard to guess the cause. "Yes, I am white," he announced in imperfect Spanish. "Your people know me as the White Apache."

The name rekindled Maria's fear. Every resident of the states of Sonora and Chihuahua had heard of the renegade known as the White Apache. He had burned many ranches and slain scores of helpless victims. It was claimed he was the worst murderer on the frontier, even worse than the Apaches with whom he rode. And she was in his clutches!

"Do you speak English?" Clay asked, still speaking Spanish.

"Yes," Maria responded in English. "A little, anyway."

In the increasing light Maria saw the rest of the band clearly for the first time. They were all full-blooded Apaches, and there was not a glimmer of compassion in the eyes of a single one. In fact, one of them glowered at her as if he wanted to wring her neck.

"Good," Clay said. "I don't get to hear it used

all that much anymore, so I'd be obliged if you'd speak English as much as possible."

There was no malice in the man's voice. Maria wondered if perhaps the rumors about him were false, if perhaps she could prevail on him to let her go. "What do you plan to do with me?"

"You can't guess?" Clay rejoined, grabbing her wrist and leading her to a flat rock, where he gestured for her to take a seat.

Maria almost refused out of sheer spite. But the Apaches were watching, and there was no predicting how they would take it if she gave them any trouble. "Please, senor," she said, easing down. "Can we talk?"

"About what?" Clay said in the act of turning.

"Me, what you are doing, and how you can become a very rich man."

"Don't tell me. You come from a rich family, and you figure your pa will be glad to fork over a king's ransom to get you back safe and sound?"

"Exactly."

"Save your breath," Clay said. "The Apaches have no use for money."

"What about you? My father will pay you in gold, not pesos—so much gold that you will need a wagon to transport it. Just think of how wealthy you would be."

"I've got news for you, lady," Clay said, and his next words surprised him as much as they dismayed her. "I don't care about being rich. There was a time, another lifetime ago, when I did. I'd have given anything to be like that hombre Midas and have so much money I couldn't count it all." Clay sighed. "Now there's only one thing

I give a damn about, and it sure as hell isn't being rich."

"What is it?" Maria probed, unwilling to accept that any American did not love money as much as life itself. Her limited experience with gringos had taught her they were all devoted to gold.

"Revenge," Clay rasped.

The fleeting hatred that contorted his features convinced Maria Gonzalez. For a few seconds she swore that she saw red-hot flames in the depths of his eyes. Or was it a trick sparked by the rising sun? she wondered, as he faced his savage companions.

Rather abruptly a horse uttered a wavering whinny that ended in a strangled grunt. Maria jerked around and saw the animal thrashing feebly on the ground, its throat slit from ear to ear. The Apache who had glowered at her was the one who slew the hapless mount, and when he lifted his head from the sickening deed, he gazed straight at her and grinned wickedly. Maria shuddered and nearly bolted.

Taggart drew his knife and moved to help butcher the horse. "We must eat and be on our way before the sun clears the horizon," he stated.

"Why are you in such a hurry?" Fiero taunted. "The *Nakai-yes* will never catch up to us. And even if they did, they will run off like scared rabbits when we turn on them."

"It is not wise to be too confident," Taggart said. "Look at what happened with the scalphunters."

He glanced at the woman, who sat slumped over, as forlorn as could be. Taggart hoped Fiero was right. Most of the time when Apaches took captives there was no pursuit at all. But something, whether intuition or a premonition, warned him that this time it would be different. This time they might have bitten off more than they could chew.

Chapter Four

Capt. Vicente Filisola felt some of the tension drain out of him when he spied a pinpoint of light over a mile away. It was the glow from a campfire at Adobe Wells. He took it as a good sign. The Apaches hadn't wiped out the Gonzalez party, as he had feared they would.

Filisola slowed from a gallop to a trot. He had pushed the patrol mercilessly for hours and all the animals could use some rest. Not to mention the men. As for Filisola, what he wanted most was the company of the charming senorita. He envisioned the two of them seated by that campfire, warmed by hot coffee and the flames of the inner passion he hoped to stoke within her.

When Adobe Wells was only a quarter of a mile off, Filisola noticed a lot of commotion. Figures kept moving back and forth in front of the fire, which struck him as peculiar. At that time of night the Gonzalez family and their vaqueros should have been resting after their hard day of travel.

Presently Filisola heard a shout and saw men swinging toward him with rifles and pistols raised. Standing in the stirrups, he hailed the camp. "Senor Gonzalez, it is Capt. Filisola. Do not shoot. My men and I are coming in."

To Filisola's amazement, none of the men lowered their weapons. Not until he came within the circle of light cast by the crackling flames did they finally relax. Right away he saw that something was dreadfully wrong. Senora Gonzalez was in tears, her shoulders shaking with sobs.

Martin Gonzalez had never been so glad to see anyone in all his life as he was to see the young officer and the soldiers. Their arrival was a godsend, he reflected, as he hurried forward and took the captain's hand in his. "You could not have come at a better time!"

Only then did Filisola spy the bodies lying beyond the fire and see several men wearing makeshift bandages. He also realized the senorita was missing. "I am too late," he said sadly, his insides becoming like ice.

"You knew we would be attacked?" Martin asked.

The captain explained about the ambush and the missing uniforms and horses.

"I see," Martin said, then went on to detail the attack on the camp and the abduction of his daughter.

"We must go after her immediately," Filisola declared. He turned to remount.

"Wait," Martin said, placing a hand on the other's arm. "We must not be impetuous, my young friend."

"How can you say that when it is your own flesh and blood those devils have taken?"

"Believe me, fear for her safety is tearing me up inside," Martin said softly so his wife would not overhear. "But it would do Maria no good for us to rush blindly off into the night. We must wait for daylight. One of my vaqueros is a skilled tracker. Once he is on a trail, not even Apaches can shake him." Martin glanced at the white lather caking the officer's mount. "Besides, your horses are on the verge of collapse. They need rest."

There was no denying that Gonzalez was right, but Filisola could hardly bear the thought of the sweet senorita in the clutches of the terrors of Mexico. His only consolation was that in all likelihood the Apaches would not kill her unless she gave them trouble. "Very well," he said reluctantly. "We will do as you request."

"At first light we will head out," Martin said. "I will send the wounded on to Janos in the carriage with my wife. She will inform my brother. And knowing how much Jose cares for his niece, it is safe to say that he will do all in his power to help us."

Vicente brightened a little. His superior, Col. Jose Gonzalez, had fought in many Indian campaigns. There was no better officer in the entire army. Unlike many commanders who were sent to frontier posts as punishment, Jose Gonzalez had requested to be sent to the hellhole called Janos because he thrived on hardship and combat.

"Yes, he will," Filisola agreed. "I wouldn't be surprised if he calls out the entire garrison. Apaches might be demons, but five of them are

50

no match for that many troopers."

For the first time in hours, both men smiled.

When faced with having to decide between the lesser of two evils, most people pick the one that will do them the least amount of harm.

Maria Gonzalez was no exception. She considered all five of her captors to be vile killers, but of the bunch of them, the American known as the White Apache was the one she feared the least. So far he had treated her roughly but courteously, which was better treatment than she would receive at the hands of the full-blooded warriors who dogged her heels. She made it a point to do her best to keep up with him and to stay close to him when they stopped, which wasn't often enough to suit her.

They had been on the go for five hours. Maria was on the verge of exhaustion. She was coated with sweat from head to toe, and her own body odor disgusted her. Her legs plodded mechanically onward mile after grueling mile, moving more out of dumb instinct than intelligent design.

Maria was not accustomed to traveling so far afoot. On the hacienda when she had to cover any great distance, she always rode or had servants transport her in a carriage. Now her legs and feet pulsed with torment with every stride she took, and she knew it was only a matter of time before they would give out on her.

The sun blazed down on the barren landscape like a golden inferno. Maria's hat had fallen off and none of her captors had bothered to replace it. Her shawl was gone too, which was a blessing since it had only made her hotter.

Maria longed for a drink or to lie down and sleep the day away. The Apaches, however, forged ever deeper into the Sierra Madre Mountains, running tirelessly. They showed no signs of being the least bit tired or thirsty or hungry. Maria mused that the stories about the red devils must be true: they were inhuman, endowed with powers no one else could hope to match. She glanced back at them, wondering what they thought of her and whether they would slay her before the day was done.

Had Maria been able to read their thoughts, she would have found the warriors held mixed feelings about her. Delgadito and Cuchillo Negro were both impressed by her stamina. It was unusual for *Nakai-yes* females to hold up well on long journeys, at least until they were properly broken in. While neither had ever taken a Mexican wife, both contemplated the merits of doing so. Neither were attracted to the captive by her looks. In their estimation she was too scrawny, more like a bird than a person, and her face was too pinched, her hair too short. They preferred a sturdy, competent, attractive Apache woman.

Fiero never gave the captive's charms a stray thought. She was a woman, and women were beneath notice in his opinion. They were put on earth for two things and two things alone: to bear children and to tend a man's wickiup. Nothing else about them was important. The only thing about this one that mattered was the foolishness of stealing her. It was a waste of their time, he figured. She would make a terrible wife.

The youngest Chiricahua, Ponce, likewise did

not give the captive much attention. It seemed in part from having lost the Apache woman he had loved. He was in no frame of mind to regard another woman with more than idle interest. As far as the captive was concerned, he had been reared to view the *Nakai-yes* with contempt. They were easy to kill, easy to plunder. Their men were as timid as rabbits, their women as useless as an extra foot. The captive was typical and did not merit any attention.

Ponce did agree that building the band up again was an excellent idea, but not with weaklings. He would have preferred going to the Chiricahua Reservation to find Apache women.

These, then, were the thoughts of the warriors regarding the woman they had abducted. Maria Gonzalez had only their inscrutable expressions to go by, and a lifetime of believing Apaches were the most bloodthirsty butchers on the face of the planet tainted her outlook. She would gaze into their dark, impassive eyes and read her death in them when they were not even thinking about her.

It was toward noon that matters came to a head. The band was making for a high pass that would see them through to the east side of the mountains. From there they would head northward into the Arizona Territory.

For the last mile or so it had been apparent to Clay that the woman was having a difficult time keeping up. He maintained a steady pace anyway in the belief that the sooner she became used to doing things the Apache way the better it would be for her.

Then, as they scaled the crest of a steep ridge,

Clay heard a low groan and a thud. He turned to find her on her side, breathing raggedly. "On your feet," he said.

"I can't," Maria puffed. An acute pain lanced her side, and her legs were leaden weight she could barely raise an inch off the earth. "Please. Let me rest a bit. Just a short while, I beg you."

The Apaches formed a semicircle around her.

"I knew she could not keep up," Fiero said scornfully. "We might as well slit her throat and leave her for the vultures and coyotes to eat."

"I agree. She will make a poor wife," Ponce said. "She is not worth the bother."

Clay planted his feet firmly at her side. "We have gone to all this trouble to bring her this far. I say we should take her the rest of the way."

Fiero motioned angrily. "She will just slow us down. She is weak, like all her kind."

"I was weak when you first found me," Clay pointed out. "If we give her a chance, she might surprise us."

Delgadito grunted. "Just so the surprise is not a knife in the back. A warrior I knew was slain in that very manner. He thought that he had tamed the woman he had stolen, but she tricked him to lower his guard and stabbed him one night while he slept."

"What happened to her?" Clay asked.

"She tried to run off but we tracked her down and brought her back. The man she stabbed cut off the fingers of her right hand so she could not use it to stab him again. He also cut her hamstring so she could not run off again. After that she was a perfect wife."

Maria listened intently although she could not

comprehend a word they said. She imagined they were discussing ways to kill her and once more appealed to the one man she felt might help her. "Please," she said. "All I need is a little time to catch my breath. Or perhaps you would consent to carry me for a while?"

"Carry you?" Clay scoffed. "Apaches never carry women or children, not even when they are sick. Stand up and keep going."

"I can't, I tell you," Maria insisted. "My legs gave out. And small wonder. I haven't done this much walking at one time in my entire life."

Fiero did not like the tone the woman used. Before Clay Taggart could stop him, he took a short step and kicked the captive in the ribs, snarling, "Get off the ground, woman, or suffer the consequences."

It annoyed Clay that Fiero saw fit to abuse the woman when he had been the one who had stolen her. "I took her, so by *Shis-Inday* custom she is mine to do with as I see fit. And I plan to keep her."

"Who are you to lecture me about our customs?" Fiero responded testily. "You are the white-eye here. I am Chiricahua."

Cuchillo Negro saw the firebrand's face harden and intervened to avert possible bloodshed. Fiero was not one to tolerate real or imagined slights and might well challenge Clay to ritual combat. "It is true that he is not of our blood, but we have accepted him as one of us. He has the right to live by our ways if he so chooses. That makes the woman his."

Fiero moved off and scanned the slopes above. There were times, such as now, when he keenly regretted ever having joined Delgadito's band. They wasted too much time on silly matters like stealing useless women when they should devote all their energy to killing their enemies.

Clay nodded at Cuchillo Negro. "Thank you," he said sincerely. Several times the laconic Apache had come to his aid in disputes involving Fiero and others, and he had yet to learn why.

"She is your woman," Cuchillo Negro said. "You must see to it that she does not slow us down."

"Yes," Delgadito said. "If she is not strong enough to hold her own, you must treat her as you would a horse that has gone lame."

"I will make her keep up," Clay said. The warriors continued on. Clay sank onto a knee and bent over the woman. "What's your name, ma'am?"

"Maria Gonzalez."

"Well, Miss Gonzalez, if you aim to go on living, you'd better light a shuck after my pards as best you're able, or you'll never live to see the night."

Maria couldn't decide if he was threatening her or warning her. Struggling to sit up, she brushed hair from her face and adopted the sort of expression that never failed to elicit the pity of any male she met. "Have a heart, senor. I have been trying my best. I just can't go on."

"Fine," Clay said and started to pull his Bowie knife.

The sight of the gleaming blade brought Maria to her feet, her heart leaping into her throat. Half expecting to be gutted, she recoiled a step.

"I don't want to have to go through this again," Clay said, shoving the Bowie back into its beaded leather sheath. He was glad he had scared her into obeying, because as much as he would hate to admit it to his Chiricahua friends, he had no desire to see any harm befall her.

Maria dutifully fell into step behind him. One of the Apaches, the warrior who scowled a lot, was sneering at her in blatant ridicule. She ignored him and concentrated on moving her tired limbs. After a while the sharp pain subsided and was replaced by a constant dull ache. To take her mind off her discomfort, she cleared her throat and said, "Do you mind if we talk?"

Clay was all set to tell her no. But the truth was that he had not talked with women in so long that he had nearly forgotten how pleasant their company could be. "Usually Apaches don't like to chatter when they're on the go, but I suppose I can make an exception in your case. What do you want to chew the cud about?"

"You," Maria said, for lack of anything else. "What is your real name?"

"Lickoyee-shis-inday."

"No, not your Apache name. I mean the name you had before you took up with them."

"Taggart. My handle was Clay Taggart."

"Was? Do you no longer consider yourself a white man?" Maria asked. She had a method to her questions. Long ago she had learned the basic lesson of dealing with the opposite sex that all women learned sooner or later, namely that men like nothing more than to talk about themselves, and that once they unburdened themselves to a woman, they regarded their confidante fondly. If she could gain his trust, she reasoned, she might be able to entice him into helping her escape.

"To be honest," Clay said, "less and less every day. The longer I'm with the Chiricahuas, the more I feel like one of them. They're the only friends I've got in the world."

Maria's interest perked up. If the gringo was that starved for friendship, she would have no problem wrapping him around her little finger. "Perhaps after a time you will regard me as your friend."

Clay had his back to her or she would have seen his grin. It amused him that so young a woman would try so obvious a ploy. "Maybe," he said.

"You mentioned before that there is only one thing you care about: revenge," Maria said, picking her words with care. "Revenge against whom."

"A sidewinder named Gillett. The son of a bitch stole my land and nearly had me doing a strangulation jig. I owe him, ma'am, owe him big. And I aim to collect."

"How did you get involved with these Apaches?"

"They saved me from Gillett. Twice over. When all my so-called white friends had turned their backs on me, the Apaches pulled my bacon out of the fire."

The revelation complicated things. Maria had assumed Taggart was just another amoral killer, just another of the deadly breed that infested northern Mexico and the southwestern part of the United States like fleas on a dog. But the man had a reason for his actions, and his loyalty to the Apaches would make gaining his help a much harder task. "I see," she said, stalling while she worked out how best to proceed.

From above them came the cry of a hunting

58

hawk. Clay glanced up at Fiero, who was pointing to the south. From their elevation a tiny cloud of dust was visible, drawing slowly nearer to the foothills.

Maria saw the dust also. "My father!" she exclaimed, clasping her hands in joy.

"If it is," Clay said, "you'd be smart to pray he doesn't get too close. My friends might take it into their heads to make sure he never finds you."

Raw terror coursed through Maria's veins. Should anything happen to her father, she was doomed. Her mother would never be able to track her down or know how to go about making an exchange. "You said that you would not accept money to ransom me. Is there nothing at all you would take? Horses? Guns? Trade goods?"

"All I want is you."

The slopes were steeper the higher they climbed. They passed the tree line and the Apaches had to avail themselves of what little cover was to be found. Maria marveled at their skill in gliding across the rugged terrain like disembodied spirits. They showed an uncanny knack for blending into the background. And the man once known as Clay Taggart was every bit their equal. She was right behind him, yet she never heard his sole scuff the ground. He seemed to have a way of setting his feet down that absorbed any noise he made.

The band crossed a gully, scaled a rock-strewn slope, and approached a towering cleft in a jagged spire of a peak crowned by an eagle's nest.

Maria was fast becoming winded. She labored for every breath and had to compel her legs to move through sheer willpower. Several times she stopped, but went on right away when Clay glared at her. She was so tired that she could barely hold her chin up. Head bobbing, she stumbled in her captor's wake. For seconds on end her eyes would close. Consequently she had no idea that Taggart had stopped until she bumped into him.

They were at the cleft. To the right shimmered a small pool of water. The Apaches were on their knees, sipping from cupped hands.

Uttering a cry of delight, Maria dashed to the spring and threw herself onto her stomach. She gulped greedily. Never had water tasted so delicious. Suddenly a hand fell on her shoulder.

"Not so fast, ma'am," Taggart said. "You'll wind up with a powerful bellyache if you don't take it easy."

Maria nodded, but could not resist drinking more. She finally sat up and looked down at herself. Her dress, which had been layered with dust and dirt, was soaked to the waist. She was a mess. Yet she didn't mind.

"We will rest a few minutes," Clay said.

"For my sake?" Maria asked, hoping he had convinced the Apaches on her behalf.

"No. My friends and I can go for long spells without water, but that doesn't mean we'll look a gift horse in the mouth. We're in no rush, ma'am. Your father is hours behind us. By morning I reckon we'll lose him for good."

Maria had to resist an insane notion to bolt down the slope. "You do not know my father like I do," she said. "He will never give up, not while he lives."

"I doubt he'll follow us all the way into Arizona," Clay said. "And once we reach our hideout in the

Chiricahua Mountains, no one will ever find us."

The prospect was too depressing to ponder. Maria splashed water on her face, then tried to smooth and clean her dress. It was hopeless.

The man known as the White Apache was reminded of the woman he had once cherished more than life itself. Lilly had been a stickler for her appearance too. He shut his mind to the memory.

Near the pool towered a boulder the size of a cabin. Maria jabbed a thumb at it and made bold to ask, "Will you excuse me for a few minutes, Senor Taggart?"

"What for?" Clay said and felt like an jackass for asking when she blushed. "Oh, sure, go ahead. Just don't try to run off. You wouldn't get far."

"I won't," Maria said. She walked around the boulder and heeded nature's call. As she straightened, a piercing shriek echoed off the peak, and the next thing she knew, something sliced into her unprotected back.

Chapter Five

The sun had not yet cleared the horizon when Martin Gonzalez and Capt. Vicente Filisola set out to rescue Martin's daughter. They waited just long enough to see the carriage off with an escort of two troopers. Theresa Gonzalez waved, her cheeks streaked by tears that she thought would never end.

Martin started the day brimming with confidence. His vaquero, Pedro, was an exceptional tracker and would eventually run the Apaches down. There were only five of the savages, and between the soldiers and his own men, he had 16 guns to rely on. It was more than enough to get the job done.

Only one thing marred Martin's outlook. He did not like to dwell on the fate worse than death that might have already befallen his darling little Maria. Apaches stole pretty young women for only one reason. He could only hope the devils would not violate her while they were fleeing back to their stronghold in the north.

Capt. Filisola shared the father's fears, but he did not voice them. He was, after all, a gentleman. In his mind's eye he kept seeing Maria, kept recalling the veiled invitation in her eyes, the promise of the fine time they might have together. It bothered him a bit that he should find himself caring so deeply for a senorita he hardly knew. In all his many conquests of the fairer half of the species, he had seldom dwelled on one woman for so long.

The officer and the father rode at the head of the column. At Filisola's suggestion, Martin had directed his vaqueros to ride in twos, as the soldiers did. Far in front of the main group rode Pedro and Sgt. Amat. The sergeant had some experience tracking but nowhere near as much as the somber vaquero.

Until the middle of the afternoon the trail was easy to follow. The Apaches had stuck to open country, and they had made good time, given that they had not had the benefit of a moon.

The sun was high in the sky when Pedro, squinting ahead at the rolling foothills that bordered the high Sierra Madres, spotted a number of dark shapes. "Damn," he spat.

"What is wrong?" Sgt. Amat asked. A career soldier, he had tangled with Apaches many times before and knew to always expect the unexpected. It would not have surprised him if the red demons sprang another ambush. He was as highly strung as piano wire, one hand resting on the carbine across his thighs.

"They are on foot now," Pedro said. "It will be

much harder from here on."

Amat rounded up the four horses while Pedro rode higher into the hills, a cocked pistol in his right hand. He came on the charred embers of a fire and beside it the carcass of a horse the Apaches had roasted. Here he waited, studying the various tracks, until his employer and the others caught up with him.

"Well?" Martin asked bluntly.

Pedro gestured toward the stark peaks that speared toward the azure sky. "They went that way, sir. Up. Your daughter is still with them and has not been harmed. At least, she does not limp or show any other sign of being hurt."

"Thank the Lord," Martin said. He nodded at the slope beyond. "Go on. But always stay in sight. If you see anything suspicious, and I mean anything, you are to stop until we catch up."

Pedro hesitated. "There is one more thing, sir. It might be important. It might not."

"What?" Martin asked impatiently.

"These tracks. I have examined them most carefully. Four are the tracks of Apaches, of that there is no doubt. But the fifth man, he is different."

"Different how?"

"He walks like an Apache but he is not an Apache."

"I do not understand," Martin said. Coming from anyone else, he would have dismissed the remark as utter nonsense, but Pedro had worked for him more than 15 years and he had learned to rely on the man's judgment.

Pedro shifted from foot to foot and stared at a print in the earth by the fire. "I know this will sound crazy, sir, but I would swear by the Virgin that the fifth man is not Apache at all. If I had to guess, I would say he is white."

"You must be mistaken," Martin said.

Capt. Filisola had been an alert listener. "Perhaps not, Senor Gonzalez," he said, his fear for Maria's safety mounting dramatically. "Have you not heard of the White Apache?"

Excited murmurs broke out among the soldiers and vaqueros. All of them were aware of the latest scourge to plague their people. All of them knew his reputation. They were no longer hunting just five Apaches, which was enough of a perilous challenge in itself. They were after a man reputed to be a living terror, a man who took delight in slaughtering innocents. A few of them crossed themselves and others uttered silent prayers for deliverance. It never occurred to any of them that the grisly stories they had heard might have been mere tall tales, the sort that spread through cantinas like wildfire.

Martin Gonzalez had heard some of the same reports, and he blanched on hearing the name. "The White Apache," he said in an awed tone. "Dear God, my poor Maria."

"We will save her," Filisola declared, wishing he felt as confident as he sounded.

Pedro cleared his throat. "It is my guess, sir, that they will cross the Sierras and then head for the border. Once they are across, they know they are safe."

"They think they will be," Martin said, "but they are wrong. If they go across the border, so will I."

"We will catch them long before they reach it,"

Filisola remarked. "They made a mistake when they abandoned their horses."

The tracker was not so sure. "Apaches can go farther on foot in one day than a man can on horseback," he reminded the officer. "And they will stick to the roughest terrain to throw us off."

Martin motioned upward. "Enough talk. We are wasting precious time. Start tracking, Pedro. We will be right behind you."

"Yes, sir."

The rescuers climbed on, a solemn air about them, while high above an eagle shrieked.

Taggart heard that same shriek, then a low cry and the sound of a scuffle. Pushing erect, he dashed around the boulder the captive had gone behind and discovered her on her knees, swatting futilely at a large eagle that had dug its curved talons into her shoulders and was pecking at her head.

Taggart sprang to her defense, swinging his rifle. The eagle ducked, screeched at him, and tried to rip open his arm. He pivoted out of harm's way. Dodging to the right, he drove the stock at the bird's side but its flailing wing deflected the blow. Meanwhile its huge talons dug deeper into Maria's back. She cried out again and fell to her hands and knees.

Clay stepped back and took aim. As if an uncanny instinct warned it that it was about to be shot, the eagle vented a high-pitched screech and flapped into the air. Once clear of the boulder, it tucked its wings and dived. It was a blur as it streaked out over the base of the mountain and then spiraled back toward the nest high overhead.

Once Clay was assured the eagle was not going to attack again, he sank down beside the captive. She was on her knees, her arms pressed to her chest. She shook uncontrollably. Blood streamed from the nasty wounds the predatory bird had inflicted.

"Why?" Maria asked through clenched teeth. "Why did it come after me?"

"I have no idea," Clay said, leaning over so he could inspect the wounds. The sun flashed off a shiny object in her hair. Gingerly, he removed a silver barrette and held it where she could see it. "My guess would be this was to blame. I think it was female. Maybe it figured you were a threat to its nest or young'uns."

"I love birds," Maria said lamely. "I would never harm one." She was in such agony that she could hardly think straight. Looking up, she saw the four Apaches observing her with stony expressions.

"We'll need to patch you up," Clay said, putting an arm around her waist to help her stand. Changing to the Apache tongue, he said, "She is badly hurt. We must make a fire so I can tend her wounds."

Fiero snorted. "She has a couple of scratches. They are not worth bothering about."

"That eagle dug its talons in deep," Clay said. "We'd do the same for you if it had gone after you instead."

"I would laugh at such wounds," Fiero said. "Apaches are not weaklings who go all to pieces when they suffer small cuts."

"There is no wood here for a fire anyway," Delgadito said. "We must move on."

"You go ahead. I'll catch up," Clay said. Without waiting to see if they would do as he wanted, he scooped Maria Gonzalez into his arms. She stiffened and made as if to strike him, but evidently thought better of the idea and let herself be carried to the pool.

Clay deposited her gently, drew the Bowie, and reached for the hem of her dress.

"What are you doing?" Maria asked anxiously.

"We need bandages, and I doubt you'd want me to use my breechcloth."

For the first time since Maria had met him, Clay smiled. She couldn't help but return the smile until she realized what she was doing and adopted a more primly proper look. "Do what you must," she said softly.

It did not take long for Clay to cut off a three-inch-wide strip and soak it in the water. Since he knew she was not about to permit him to apply the bandage under her dress, he did so on the outside, wrapping it around her body and tying it under her right arm. It made a poor compress and hardly stanched the flow of blood, but it was the best he could do at the moment.

"Let's go," Clay said, offering his hand as he rose.

Maria balked, but just for a few moments. She accepted his help and stood. Her legs nearly buckled, catching her by surprise, and she would have fallen had her captor not caught her.

"I'll carry you, ma'am."

"No, I can manage," Maria assured him. She

felt the heat of his body against hers and abruptly became aware of the raw, animal power radiating from the man. That power was like a physical force, and it spawned disturbing sensations deep within her. She pushed back and shuffled toward the far end of the pass, glad for the cool breeze that buffeted the rocky defile.

For his part, Clay was trying to control similar feelings kindled by their brief contact. It had been so long since a woman's warm breath had fanned his face that hers set his blood afire. He would have liked to have jumped into the pool and stayed there until he cooled down. It angered him that he was acting like a randy schoolboy, yet there was nothing he could do about it.

The Apaches were hundreds of yards away, moving in single file as was their custom. In the lead walked Delgadito, a rare smirk creasing his lips. He was pleased beyond measure that Clay wanted to build up the band again. It had been Delgadito's plan to do so all along. And once the band was big enough to suit him, he would wrest leadership from Clay, at the point of a knife if he had to, and reclaim his rightful position as a leader of the Chiricahuas.

The dull crack of a shod hoof on rock brought Delgadito up short. Immediately he flattened against the stone wall of the pass, listening. The sound had come from the east side of the mountain.

Delgadito glanced around. His companions had also stopped, and they were staring at him, ready to follow his lead just as they had done in the days before the scalphunters wiped out the old band.

"Fiero," Delgadito whispered.

The most bloodthirsty Chiricahua who had ever lived padded forward to the end of the pass and halted in the shadow of a rock monolith. From his vantage point he could see the many slopes below and to either side. Less than 200 yards off, winding up a serpentine animal trail, were six Mexicans. The incline was so steep that they were walking their mounts.

All six wore sombreros and grungy clothes. All six had bandoleers crisscrossing their chests, and each wore two guns, tied down for fast draws. They had the haggard aspect of men who had traveled for many days, and the last one in line kept looking over his shoulder as if to spot pursuers.

Fiero pegged them as ruthless scavengers who preyed on anyone and everyone, much as Apaches did, but who did so for the most base of motives: greed. Apaches could never understand why some whites and Mexicans killed for dollars and pesos when there were so many grander reasons, like revenge and warring on one's enemies.

If there were an official Apache creed, it was to steal without being caught and to kill without being slain. Those were the precepts by which every Chiricahua lived, and none did so more fervently than Fiero. The moment he set eyes on the bandits, his agile brain was working out a way to kill them without being killed in order to steal their horses and possessions.

Whirling, Fiero raced to his friends and reported what he had seen, adding, "They will reach the pass soon. If we are to act, it must be now."

"But what about *Lickoyee-shis-inday?*" Cuchillo Negro asked. "He must be warned."

"We do not have the time," Fiero said.

Behind them, Clay wondered why the four Apaches suddenly sprinted for the mouth of the pass. Were they leaving him behind on purpose? He would not put it past Fiero or Ponce, but he rated Delgadito a close friend and doubted that Cuchillo Negro would desert him under any circumstances.

"Where are they going, senor?" Maria asked.

"Beats me," Clay said. "Maybe they're tired of my company."

Maria was quick to exploit the opening. "If they care so little for you, why do you stay with them?"

"I told you before. They're my pards."

"Perhaps it is time you found new pards," Maria said. "What have they done for you but get you into trouble with the law? Or do you like being a wanted man on both sides of the border? Do you like being hated more than the Apaches themselves?"

"You keep missing the point, little lady. They'll do to ride the river with."

"What does that mean?"

"That I've thrown in with them, come what may. If I can help them take back the land stolen by my government, I will. After all they've done for me, I owe them that much."

"So you are saying you have a debt of honor?"

"Something like that, I reckon," Clay said.

The warriors had disappeared out the end of the pass, and he picked up the pace to learn why. Maria was dragging her heels, so he snatched her wrist and hauled her along, heedless of the pained look she adopted.

"What is the matter with you? You are hurting me."

"Tough molasses," Clay said. He was tired of her trying to turn him against the Chiricahuas, and figured it was about time she learned who the leader of the band was.

Clay was 20 feet from the opening when he heard the nicker of a horse. Instantly he dropped low, his senses primed like a mountain lion's, his mind empty of all save the matter at hand. In an instant, he had changed his mental attitude from that of a gruff rancher to that of a wary Apache. His posture, his movements, and his whole attitude were more Indian than white. He had became as much like a Chiricahua as the Chiricahuas themselves.

Clay crept closer to the sunlight. There was no sign of the warriors. He could tell that a number of horses were nearing the pass. Flattening, he let go of Maria and snaked to the edge of the shelf. He did not know what to expect but he was surprised to see six bandits a score of yards away. At the front was a giant bearded man who had a belly the size of a washtub.

Clay turned to take Maria into hiding, but as he twisted to the right, she sped past him on the left. Her slender arms overhead, her hair flying, she shouted at the top of her lungs in Spanish, "Help me! Help me! For the love of God! I have been stolen by Apaches! They are all around you!"

The bandits were riveted in place for several seconds, too startled to do more than gape. The one in the lead came to life quickest, clawing

72

out his pistols and growling orders to those behind him.

Clay rose to try to stop Maria before she reached the bandits. But the leader saw him and opened fire, banging off shot after shot. Clay had to drop down again as slugs chipped at the shelf.

A war whoop wavered on the wind. A rifle blasted. Pistols cracked in cadence in reply, mingled with lusty curses and the frantic neighing of mounts.

Clay rose high enough to see the battle raging below. About 15 feet down, the Chiricahuas had hidden among boulders on either side of the animal trail. They would have ambushed the unsuspecting bandits had Maria Gonzalez not ruined everything. She was past the boulders, streaking for the bandits, some of whom were trying to climb on their animals while others blasted at the warriors.

Extending his Winchester, Clay fixed the front bead on the chest of the bandit leader. As his finger curled around the trigger, the leader's horse, trying to flee, yanked the man off balance. His shot missed.

Another bandit had a boot in a stirrup and was rising into the saddle when a slug slammed into his spine between the shoulder blades. He stiffened, clutched at his back, and toppled. The riderless horse, spooked, fled down the trail, colliding with other animals.

Cuchillo Negro broke from cover, going after the woman. A hail of gunfire drove him to ground.

Realizing he must act or lose Maria, Clay

launched himself into a roll that sent him over the rim and down the slope toward the boulders. He leaped to his feet before he stopped rolling and gained shelter as one of the bandits peppered his vicinity.

When Clay popped up to fire, he saw the leader in the saddle and Maria clambering up behind the man. Again he aimed, and again he was thwarted when the leader wheeled the horse and galloped madly down the slope, barreling past another bandit who was trying to climb on a frightened animal that wouldn't stand still.

Clay jumped up and tried to settle his sights on the leader's head, but Maria's was too close. He might hit her by mistake.

The last of the bandits had managed to mount. Hugging his saddle, he fled, firing blindly over a shoulder.

Rather than waste ammunition, the warriors stopped firing and came into the open.

Clay started down the trail. The horse of the slain bandit had been unable to run off because its reins were looped around the dead man's wrist and he wanted to get to it before it pulled free.

"Where are you going, *Lickoyee-shis-inday?*" Delgadito asked.

"After her," Clay answered without slowing.

"Wait," Cuchillo Negro said.

Against his better judgment, Clay paused. "What is it? I must hurry if I am to catch them."

"Why bother?" Cuchillo Negro said. "There are five of them and only one of you. They will be expecting someone to come after them."

"Does my brother imply I cannot handle five *Nakai-yes?*" Clay said.

74

Bloodbath

"These are not ordinary Mexicans. They are killers, mad wolves who attack in packs. Let them have the woman. We can always find another to replace her."

"I want this one," Clay said and raced on. "Head north. If all goes well I will meet you at Caliente Springs. Wait for me as long as you can."

He heard Delgadito call his name, but did not stop. The bandit's horse shied and tried to pull away from him until he had the reins in hand and spoke to it softly. At length it permitted him to fork leather.

Dust raised by the fleeing bandits still hung in the air. Clay wound down the trail into scrub pines. Here the wily outlaws had veered into the trees, bearing to the southeast. He glued himself to their tracks and presently glimpsed them about half a mile ahead of him, riding hell bent for leather.

Since Clay did not want them to spot him, he moved into thicker timber and slowed. There was no need to ride his horse into the ground. He could not wrest Maria from them until they stopped.

Clay had not thought to count the riders he saw. He did so when he reached a clearing and glimpsed them a second time. It puzzled him to spy only four where there should be five. He did not know what to make of the missing man. Then he came to the barren slope of a gulch the bandits had crossed, and he descended. Too late he spotted the glint of sunlight off metal. The next second a rifle boomed.

Chapter Six

Col. Jose Gonzalez was widely known as one of the bravest officers in all of Mexico. Those who knew him personally were also aware that he was one of the most vain.

On this particular day, the colonel stood in front of the full-length mirror that adorned the inner panel of the closet door in his office at the presidio of Janos. He had on a new uniform, which had arrived the previous day from Mexico City, and he was admiring the neatly pressed shirt with its many shiny buttons and the decorations he had won for his valorous service to his country.

The colonel overlooked the fact that his hairline had receded to a point above his small ears and that his stocky frame was more like that of a hardworking farmer's than the ideal of slim military perfection. In his mind he was flawless, as grand a warrior who ever lived.

Bloodbath

A commotion erupted outside. Col. Gonzalez heard a shout, then more yells followed by the drumming of hooves. Donning his hat, he sucked in his gut, clasped his hands behind his wide back, and stalked out to learn the cause of the uproar.

A number of junior officers and dozens of soldiers were clustered around someone near the hitching post. The moment Col. Gonzalez appeared in the doorway, one of those officers, Capt. Mora, snapped to attention and bellowed loud enough to be heard in town, "Commander!" Instantly the assembled soldiers fell in line.

Col. Gonzalez moved among them to the center of the cluster. Two exhausted horses were there, both lathered with enough sweat to drown an ox. Legs quivering, blowing noisily through their nostrils, they appeared ready to keel over at any second.

The soldier who had ridden them in was in scarcely better shape. His uniform was drenched, his face slick. His skin was red from the heat and he was having a hard time keeping his eyes open. The private was doing his utmost to stand at attention, even though his legs quaked worse than those of the two animals.

One of the abilities that made Gonzalez such an outstanding officer was his phenomenal memory. It was rumored that he never forgot a face or a name, and he often amazed casual acquaintances he had not seen in years by remembering the least little detail about them.

On this occasion Col. Gonzalez sorted through the file of his uncanny memory until he found the face of the soldier in front of him. "Pvt. Batres. You were sent out on patrol with Capt. Filisola, were you not? Explain yourself."

The private hiked his shoulders a hair higher and went to speak, but could not. He coughed a few times, then croaked, "I am sorry, Colonel. I have ridden over seventy miles to get here to report—" His voice broke, and he coughed more violently.

Col. Gonzalez glanced at Capt. Mora and snapped his fingers. In moments a canteen was produced. The colonel himself gave it to the private.

"Swallow small mouthfuls."

Batres did so although it was plain to all assembled that he wanted to gulp the canteen dry. He lowered it after a few sips and gratefully handed it back. "Thank you, sir. I could not have gone much longer without water."

"Your report, Private."

"Yes." Batres snapped to attention again. "I regret to inform you that our patrol was ambushed by Apaches."

The colonel took the news in stride. Apache attacks were common occurrences, and he had steeled himself to losing over a dozen men a year, on average, to the devils'. "Are you the only survivor?"

"No, sir," Batres went on hastily. "Only half the patrol was slain. The captain then led us on a forced ride to Adobe Wells—"

"Why would he go there?" Col. Gonzalez asked. "He should have gone on to Hermosillo and sent a dispatch to me."

"Capt. Filisola was worried about your brother and his family," Batres said.

Fear gripped Gonzalez. His brother was due to

arrive any day for his annual visit. "What about them?" he demanded urgently.

"We had passed them shortly before the attack. Capt. Filisola figured out that the Apaches were going after them, dressed in uniforms the savages took from our dead. He was very concerned for your brother's safety."

"You've already made that clear. Get to the point. What happened?"

"We reached Adobe Wells too late. The Apaches had already struck. Several of your brother's vaqueros were killed, and—" Private Batres hesitated, afraid to be the bearer of bad tidings.

"Out with it, man!"

"The Apaches took your niece, Colonel."

There was a collective intake of breath by the gathered troopers. Every man there knew what it meant to live under the constant nightmare of Apache raids. Every man there sympathized with their commanding officer. Furthermore, many of them had seen Maria Gonzalez. She was one of the few women permitted on the post and a vision of loveliness many secretly adored.

Batres went on in the stunned silence. "Capt. Filisola and your brother went after the Apaches. Pvt. Iberry and I were sent to escort the carriage bringing Senora Gonzalez. A wheel broke soon after we left the captain. Since there were enough men to protect the senora, I came on ahead with two horses, riding them in turns to make the trip without stopping. I thought you should know what had happened as soon as possible."

The soldiers turned their attention to their commanding officer. It was common knowledge that the colonel was a stickler for following orders.

Any man in violation was subject to the strictest possible punishment. But it was also common knowledge that the colonel appreciated initiative and rewarded those who showed loyalty above and beyond the call of duty. They waited to see which would be the case in this instance.

Col. Gonzalez had his surging emotions under control. He fixed his iron stare on the private and asked, "So Capt. Filisola did not order you to ride on ahead by yourself?"

Batres gulped. "No, sir. My orders were to stay with the carriage. But when it broke down, I thought—"

Gonzalez held up his right hand, silencing the man. "Nevertheless, you did not obey your superior. And you know that failure to follow orders must always be punished."

"Yes, sir," Batres said, crestfallen.

"As your punishment, I confine you to bed rest for three days—"

"Bed rest?" the private asked in astonishment.

"You are suffering from heatstroke, so you are not to leave your bed except for meals. I will have the doctor attend to you to make sure your recovery is swift, Sergeant."

It took a moment for the colonel's last word to register. "You called me a sergeant, Colonel. I have not even made corporal yet."

"As commander I can promote who I like when I like," Col. Gonzalez said stiffly. "As of this moment, you jump two grades to sergeant. I expect to see your uniform reflect your new rank the next time I see you."

"Yes, sir!" Batres responded, and there wasn't

Bloodbath

a man present who didn't envy him.

"Furthermore, after I return, you are assigned to my personal staff. Report to me in person."

"Yes, sir."

"Now get to the infirmary, then to bed."

The private snapped a salute and turned about. He took only three steps when his legs gave out. Several soldiers cushioned his fall and carted him off.

Col. Gonzalez stomped onto the porch fronting the headquarters building and pivoted. "You heard him. The Apaches have abducted the sweetest senorita who ever lived. Are we going to let them get away with it?"

"No, sir!" roared from 40 mouths.

"Capt. Mora," Gonzalez snapped. "Assign fifty men to guard the presidio. Have one hundred and fifty mounted and ready to depart within half an hour. Full field rations and forty extra rounds of ammunition are to be given each man. Understood?"

"Yes, sir."

The colonel marched into his office and sat down to compose a dispatch to his superiors explaining his actions and requesting that 50 soldiers be sent from Hermosillo to reinforce the Janos garrison until his return. He noticed that his hand shook slightly as he wrote, and he honestly couldn't tell if it was because of his outrage over the kidnapping of his niece or the heady thrill he always felt before going into combat against his lifelong enemies.

Either way, the Apaches responsible were going to pay for their atrocity in blood.

* * *

In the second that elapsed between the moment Clay saw the glint of sunlight and the rifle of the concealed bandit blasted, he threw himself from the saddle, diving to the right into high weeds that choked the side of the gulch. He hit on his shoulder and rolled a few yards to make it harder for the bushwhacker to pinpoint his position.

Two more slugs sheared into the vegetation but wide of where Clay lay on his belly. Rising onto his knees, he watched his mount race in panic down the gully. Without that horse his chances of overtaking the bandits were slim. He took off after it, weaving as he ran, keeping brush and trees between himself and the rifleman.

Shots cracked on the opposite rim. Twigs and branches were splintered by slugs. One nicked Clay's shin. He halted behind a pine to return fire, levering off five shots in swift succession. The gunfire from the other side ceased.

Clay ran on. The horse had disappeared around a bend in the gully. He hoped it would slow down soon or stop. But when he reached the bend, the spooked animal was hundreds of yards away with its mane flying and tail high.

"Damn!" Clay said. Crouching, he zigzagged to the far slope and up to the top. He was surprised that the bandit did not try to pick him off.

The clatter of hooves on stone told Clay why. The bandit was fleeing too. Clay streaked toward the sound, over a knoll and across a narrow flat to a rocky spine 60 feet long. He leaped onto the smooth incline, braced his heels, and scrambled to the top.

Just in time. The bandit was relying on the

spine to cover his flight and was moving along it with his body bent low over his saddle horn so he could not be seen from the gully.

Clay set down his Winchester, coiled his legs, waited until the rider came underneath him, and pounced. He wanted the man alive so he could force him to reveal the destination of the gang.

The bandit spotted Clay's shadow and jerked around, but he was too late. Clay's left shoulder rammed into the rider's side, spilling them both onto the ground. Clay regained his feet sooner and lashed out with a fist. The bandit handily jumped aside and went for one of the pistols decorating his waist.

Shifting, Clay slid in close and clamped a hand on the outlaw's wrist so the man couldn't bring the pistol into play. For hectic moments they danced in circles, each struggling for possession of the revolver. Clay forked a foot behind the man's leg and shoved, upending him. Clay landed on top, gouging his knees into the other's stomach.

A boot walloped Clay. He landed on his right shoulder next to the bandit, who redoubled his attempt to use the pistol. Clay had to strain to hold the barrel at bay. In their rolling and thrashing they smashed into the rocky spine. Clay, distracted for a heartbeat, felt a knee drive into his groin. Weakness and fleeting nausea came over him.

The bandit shoved free and jumped to his feet. Sneering in triumph, he pointed the pistol and thumbed back the hammer.

Clay snapped his left foot into the man's knee. A loud crack sounded a fraction of a second before the pistol went off. The slug thudded into the dirt inches from Clay's ear. Flipping to the left, he heard the gun thunder again but fortunately the wobbly bandit missed.

Abruptly reversing direction, Clay plowed into the bandit's legs. The Mexican staggered backward into the rock wall and cursed as his fractured knee buckled and he toppled forward, directly onto Clay.

In an instant, Clay swept both knees to his chest so that the bandit fell against the soles of his feet. Then with a heave, he hurled the man back against the spine with such force that the bandit slumped to the ground.

Clay rose. The man's pistol had fallen. He promptly picked it up. Drawing back his other hand, he gave the bandit a ringing slap across the cheek. The man started, blinked, and went motionless with fear.

"Where are the others going?" Clay asked in Spanish. To spur an answer, he cocked the pistol and pressed the end of the barrel against the tip of the man's nose.

"I don't know," the bandit said.

"Liar."

"I swear!" the man cried. "We were on our way to Hermosillo when your band attacked us. Now my amigos are running for their lives, and I have no idea where they are headed."

"I want the truth."

"That is the truth. By all that is holy, you must believe me."

"I don't," Clay said, straightening up. He smiled at the man, then shot him through the right shoulder.

Bloodbath

The shriek of torment the bandit let out with must have carried for half a mile. The man arched his spine and writhed about for a minute like a stricken wildcat, his teeth clenched, beads of sweat lining his brow.

"I would not lie again, if I were you," Clay said. "It is not hard to figure out what happened. Every outlaw gang has a leader, and yours is that big hombre with the gut. He wanted you to delay anyone who was on your trail. And he would have told you where to meet your amigos later." Clay paused and leaned down so the pistol was trained on the bandit's chest. "Where?"

The bandit licked his spittle-flecked lips, his gaze riveted on the six-shooter. "Honest to God, I do not want to die. I would tell you if we had set up a rendezvous. But there was no time. We were in too much of a hurry."

Clay lowered the pistol. There was a chance the man was actually telling the truth. He would have to do the job the hard way, by tracking the bandits. Turning, he stared at the man's horse, which had halted about 50 feet away to graze. Out of the corner of his eye, he watched the bandit. He knew what the man would do before the man did it. So when the outlaw slipped a hand onto the other pistol, he was ready.

In a smooth, fluid spin, Clay swung around and fanned the hammer twice. It was a trick few men mastered because of the tendency of a heavy-caliber pistol to kick when fired, but with practice, a skilled gunman could fan accurately at short ranges. And Clay Taggart was very skillful. Both slugs ripped into the bandit's heart, dead center. The man died without uttering another sound.

"Idiot," Clay said as he squatted to strip off the twin gunbelts the man wore. After strapping them around his waist, he loaded both pistols and slipped the bandit's bandoleers over his own chest. He retrieved the Winchester before hurrying to the sorrel, which gave him a wary scrutiny, but did not run off.

Forking leather, Clay pulled out the bandit's rifle, a Henry in excellent condition. He decided to keep it and shoved it back into the boot. Clucking the sorrel into a trot, he placed his Winchester across his legs.

A man could never have enough guns.

Martin Gonzalez felt his mouth go dry from apprehension. He looked at Pedro and asked, "You are sure of this?"

"Yes, sir," the tracker answered, motioning at the tracks behind the huge boulder. "Your daughter came behind here by herself. Then something happened. I do not know what. But she bled badly and was carried off by the White Apache."

Capt. Filisola frowned. "The ruthless butcher must have stabbed her."

Pedro cocked his head. "I do not think so, Captain. All his tracks are on top of the blood. From what I can tell, he came running, as if to help her. Then he carried her back. The four Apaches came over, but stood back, doing nothing."

"Why was she bleeding?" Martin asked, clenching his fists in frustration. "What could have happened?"

"The tracks do not tell me," Pedro said. "I am sorry, sir."

Martin led the way to the spring, where the rest of the men were watering the horses. A vaquero offered him a canteen and he took it and drank without being aware that he was doing so. All he could think of was his beloved Maria.

"How soon before we catch them?" Capt. Filisola asked the tracker.

"I cannot say. Perhaps tomorrow sometime if they stop for the night."

"Tomorrow!" Filisola said. "It might as well be next week. We must push even harder if we are to save the senorita. Can you track by torchlight? It would permit us to travel on through the night."

"It is very hard to do," Pedro said. "I might lose the trail, and I would not like to risk that."

Sgt. Amat, standing nearby, overheard and said, "If I may be so bold, sir, we must also think of the horses. They are very tired. Pressing on until morning would exhaust them. Then how will we catch the savages?"

"We will go on foot, if need be," Filisola said crisply. He disliked having his judgment questioned.

Martin removed his sombrero and mopped a hand across his forehead. "No, we won't. It is my daughter they took, and I say that we will make camp once it is too dark for Pedro to track. We all need a good night's rest."

Filisola disagreed strongly, but made no objection. Martin was a civilian and as such Filisola had the right, under Mexican law, to require the rancher to do as he wished. But Martin was also the colonel's brother, and the colonel would not take kindly to having his brother treated like a common peon.

The rescue party rode on through the pass. They were almost to the east opening when three gunshots shattered the stillness; they were the signal that Pedro had found something of interest.

Martin spurred his horse into the sunlight. The tracker and the sergeant were scouring a game trail below. Near them was a body partially hidden by small boulders. Fearing the worst, Martin galloped to the spot and could not hide his relief when he discovered it was a dead stranger, not Maria.

"What now?" Capt. Filisola asked. Dismounting, he turned the body over and examined the fleshy features. "I know this man. His name is Sesma. He is a bandit who rode with that pig, Vargas."

"Vargas and his men fought the Apaches, then fled," Pedro said.

"That sounds like Vargas," Filisola said. "He is a coward who is all too willing to kill innocents, but he runs if his own life is in danger. Col. Gonzalez claims that Vargas is the very worst of his breed—a filthy cockroach who has murdered many men, women, and children. It is too bad the Apaches did not do us a favor and wipe his gang out."

Martin saw his vaquero's features become downcast. "What is the matter, Pedro?"

"I have bad news to relay, sir."

Martin did not know what could possibly be worse than having his daughter in the clutches of vile Apaches. "Out with it."

Pedro hunkered down and touched a single

slim footprint at the side of the trail. "I think Maria was taken by this Vargas and his men."

The revelation shocked everyone into silence. Martin climbed down and inspected the track for himself. He saw where the ground near it had been chewed up by hoofprints when a horse turned to flee. "Can it really be?"

"I am afraid so. She ran to the bandits. You can see her tracks there. And this horse, when it rode off, was carrying double. See how deep the tracks are, compared to the others?"

"Dear God," Capt. Filisola said. Apaches were bad enough, but at least they would keep Maria alive to become the wife of one of their warriors. Bandits were another story entirely. Vargas killed women as readily as most men killed insects. He had also tortured and raped many of them. Maria was much worse off now than she had been before.

"Maybe she did not know these men were bandits," Pedro said. "Maybe she thought they were her only hope of escaping the Apaches."

Martin Gonzalez bowed his head in abject despair. "My poor, poor Maria! Where have the bandits taken her? What will they do to her?"

There was no answer, other than a chill gust of wind that moaned down off the mountain.

Chapter Seven

It had seemed like a good idea at the time.

When Maria Gonzalez had seen the six men approaching the pass, she had gone giddy with joy. They were Mexicans! Her own kind! Men who would help her. Men who would save her from the Apaches.

So without thinking, Maria had bolted past the White Apache and down the trail toward the burly man who led the six. She had shouted to alert them to their peril and been overjoyed when she'd reached the leader without taking a bullet in the back.

The events happened so quickly that Maria was astride the man's horse and fleeing down the mountain before she could collect her wits. Rather belatedly she realized that the man who had rescued her smelled badly. Besides that, he had a harsh air about him, even more cruel than that of the Apaches. His beady eyes actually

Bloodbath

scared her when he glanced back a few times as if to assure himself that she was indeed there.

And the man was a coward. When she was running toward him, she had seen his terror of the Apaches, a cringing terror the likes of which her father and uncle would never display.

They were bandits, Maria realized, and her heart sank within her. The horror stories she had heard about bandits rivaled those about Apaches. Having lived the sheltered life of a pampered senorita, she had never seen either until this fateful trip, and she hoped to high heaven she never saw either again, provided she lived long enough to get to somewhere safe.

Because there was nothing else to hang onto, Maria had to grasp the big man's bandoleers to keep from losing her balance on his mount. The man rode with reckless abandon, swerving wildly through tracts of trees and taking the slopes of gullies at breakneck speed. They were lucky the horse didn't break a leg and throw them both.

Then the leader reined up. But he stopped only long enough to tell one of his men to keep an eye on their back trail and bushwhack anyone who showed. The other bandit wasn't happy about being the one picked to cover their flight, but evidently his fear of the bandit leader was greater than his fear of the Apaches because he agreed and climbed down.

The big leader lashed his horse and they galloped along for over an hour, until they were well off the mountain and out on the desert to the east. The man had an amazing knack for finding gulches and arroyos through which to travel. It was as if he knew the lay of the land as well as he knew the lines in the palms of his hands.

Finally, when Maria was so tired and sore that she worried she would collapse and fall, the leader drew rein again in a dry wash rimmed by dry brush. There was a small spring, as close to dry as a spring could be and still be worthy of the name. The leader jumped down, dropped to his knees, and guzzled the water like a hog at the trough. Only after he had downed his fill did he let the rest of the bandits and the horses drink.

Maria, meanwhile, moved to one side, waiting her turn at the water. She craved a drink more than anything, but she did not care to get too close to her rescuers. In the back of her mind she hoped against hope they would simply ride on and leave her. But that feeble hope was dashed by the look the leader gave her, his hungry eyes roving over her as might the eyes of a starving man over a sumptuous feast.

The man hooked his thick thumbs in his gun belts and strutted over. His eyes glittered. Planting his dirty boots in front of her, he scratched his beard, then said, "I am Vargas, little one."

Maria kept her face as blank as a slate board, but her stomach churned. She had heard of this Vargas, a despicable killer whose list of innocent victims was longer than both her arms lined end to end. "You sound as if I should know the name," she said politely.

Vargas thumped his chest with a brawny fist. "Everyone in Mexico has heard of me."

"I haven't," Maria said, hoping he would believe her lie. She was not about to feed his exaggerated sense of self-importance and have him take the liberties he was sure to take if she showed that she was the least bit afraid of him. Her best bet was to keep him off guard and perhaps to persuade him to take her to safety despite himself.

"You must have," Vargas said. "From Ciudad Juarez to Cancun, from Mazatlan to Tampico, they know the name of Vargas."

"All I know is that you are the man who has saved me from the Apaches, and for that I am very grateful," Maria said, keeping her voice level. She had an idea that might result in her being reunited with her parents, and she put it into effect by saying, "My father will pay you a king's ransom for returning me to him—more money than you can carry in both your saddlebags."

The man's greed was as obvious as the oversize nose on his face. "Your father is rich?"

"Yes."

"What is his name?"

Maria took a few seconds to think. If she made up any old name, he might suspect she was lying. But if she revealed the truth, there was a chance Vargas had heard of her father and would take her at her word. "Martin Gonzalez."

"I know of him," Vargas said. "He has one of the largest ranches in all of Mexico. And his vaqueros are some of the toughest."

"Will you take me to my parents?" Maria asked. "I give you my word that you will be handsomely paid."

The bandit pursed his coarse lips and stroked his greasy mustache. "I must talk this over with my men."

"What is there to talk about?" Maria asked. "Surely you can use the money? And all you have to do to earn it is take me to my parents. There will be no questions asked, I assure you."

"We must talk," Vargas said and moved over to where the other bandits were huddled.

Maria took the opportunity to go to the spring. The water had been muddied by the men and the horses, but she had to quench her thirst. Cupping her right hand, she sipped gingerly, swirling the water to dilute the mud before each mouthful. The water tasted awful but it was cool and refreshing. When a shadow fell across her, Maria had to bite her lip. She refused to show her fear of the five bandits who approached her.

"Have you made up your minds?" she asked casually.

"We have," Vargas said. "And you will not like our decision."

Maria put both hands on the ground and tensed her leg muscles. If they intended to violate her, she would resist them to her dying breath. "What is it?"

Vargas grinned, exposing a black gap where four of his upper front teeth had once been. "We all know of your father. A few times we tried to steal some of his cattle but his damned vaqueros drove us off. He would not hesitate to kill any of us if we were to somehow fall into his hands. So it would be stupid of us to take you to him."

"But I give you my word—"

The bandit leader laughed. "Your word is not enough for us to risk our lives"—he paused and scratched under an armpit—"especially when we happen to also know that your father is the brother of Col. Jose Gonzalez. The good colonel has been after us for many years. He has vowed to spit on our graves one day."

Bloodbath

"But you can take me directly to our ranch," Maria said. "That way you will go nowhere near the presidio."

"I think not," Vargas said, leering. "Why do you think I have lasted as long as I have? I never take chances I do not need to take. And I do not need to take you back to your dear parents to make lots of money."

"What do you mean?"

"There are men who will pay many thousands of dollars for a pretty senorita like you."

"What kind of men?" Maria said, resisting the panic that threatened to engulf her. She knew the answer but she asked anyway to buy precious time. She had to think her way out of the terrible predicament her rash action had placed her in.

"The Comanches to the north pay in silver and gold for women such as you," Vargas said. "And there are slavers on the coast who would drool at the sight of such a lovely young thing."

Forgetting herself, Maria said, "What manner of pig are you that you would subject a woman to such a fate? Have you no decency at all?"

The leader's beady eyes glittered like the tips of bullets. "It is not very smart, senorita, for you to insult the man who has your life in the palm of his hand. But I will forgive you this time. You are too valuable to us for me to slap you around. However, a word to the wise. I will not be so merciful if you make the same mistake again."

Some of the bandits laughed the hard, brittle laughter of men who did not know the meaning of compassion or honor. In that brief moment when they were distracted, Maria made her move. She darted between two of them and ran to the nearest horse. The heavy tread of footsteps behind her lent speed to her feet.

Maria vaulted into the saddle on the fly. A hand clutched at her leg but she jabbed her heels into the bay and it broke into a gallop, heading back down the dry wash. Curses and shouts laced the air.

At the first bend, Maria looked back. The bandits were all after her, Vargas in the lead, two of them riding double. She flailed the reins to get her mount to go faster but it was already going as fast as it could.

Once around the corner, Maria reined to the right and went up the sharp incline. Loose dirt and stones spewed out from the animal's flying hooves. For a few seconds she fretted that the horse would lose its footing and crash to the bottom of the wash, but it made it up and out. She rode across the flatland, bearing eastward since in that direction she would find the nearest towns and settlements.

When next Maria checked over a shoulder, she was appalled to see Vargas gaining on her. His big black horse moved over the ground as if it had wings. She regretted that she had not taken it instead of the one she was on. Vargas, being the bandit leader, would naturally have kept the best horse of the many they had stolen.

Maria settled down to a grim race for her life and honor. For several years she had sought out the company of handsome men as discreetly as a maiden should, dating and dancing to her heart's content. It flattered her to no end that she was sought after by some of the most eligible bachelors in Mexico. But at no time during her

Bloodbath

many dates had Maria allowed any man to claim the prize that would be her husband's by virtue of their marriage.

The horse she rode seemed to sense her fear and exhibited stamina she would not have guessed that it possessed. Yet even though the animal gave its all, Vargas caught her.

It happened as Maria was going flat out on a baked stretch of earth, her hair whipping in the wind, her dress hiked well above her knees. She heard the growing drum of hooves as the bandit's horse came closer and closer.

"No!" Maria cried and tried again to spur her horse into performing a miracle. Something snatched at her dress and she shifted to see Vargas a few yards from her, bent forward so he could grab hold. She yanked her leg forward, causing him to miss. Cursing, he pulled nearer, his outstretched fingers inches away.

Frantically Maria cut to the left, gaining ground, but not for long. Vargas wore a mask of fury as he gradually overtook her.

Maria suddenly realized there was a rifle in the saddle boot. She gripped the stock and heaved, but not quite hard enough to pull the rifle all the way out. Before she could heave a second time, Vargas was at her side. His hand flicked out and closed on the rifle. He pulled, but she clung on until he was pulling so hard his face had turned red. Then she let go.

It was a clever ruse, and more was the pity that it failed to work. Vargas was flung backward and almost fell. With the tenacity of a gorilla clinging to a tree limb, he clung to his saddle horn and righted himself. And now he had the rifle.

Maria hunched low, resuming her flight. She dreaded being shot, but no bullets rang out. The only possible reason chilled her to the core. The bandits did not want damaged goods. They wanted her in one piece so she would fetch a higher price when she was sold to the Comanches or the slavers.

For the third time Vargas narrowed the gap; he was right beside her. Maria swung her fist in vain. All he did was cackle as if at the antics of a child.

"Stupid bitch!" he said.

Maria saw the Winchester barrel sweep toward her head but there was nothing she could do. She had no time to duck, no time to turn her horse, no time to do anything other than brace herself a fraction of an instant before the barrel slammed into her temple.

Pinwheels of light exploded before Maria's eyes. Pain such as she had never known lanced her from ear to ear. A black cloud engulfed her, smothering the pinwheels, and the last sensation she experienced before the cloud claimed her consciousness was that of flying through the air.

The dust raised by over 200 horses was enough to choke the air for half a mile behind the long column of soldiers and pack animals.

At the forefront rode Col. Jose Gonzalez in full dress uniform, a glistening saber at his side, a shiny new pistol in his holster. He rode a white pacer that put the other horses to shame with its high-spirited gait. His saddle, unlike the plain rigs of the troopers, was adorned with enough silver to start a mine. He was a glorified image of spit and polish, and Jose Gonzalez reveled in it.

The column was hours out of Janos, on a winding road that would bring them in due course to the Sierra Madre Mountains, well north of the Janos to Hermosillo road.

Capt. Mora, one of the six junior officers who followed the colonel, had noticed that fact. "Permission to speak, Colonel."

"Granted," Gonzalez said, his gaze never leaving the six point men a quarter of a mile out.

"Since your brother was attacked at Adobe Wells, shouldn't we be going there?"

"And why would we do that, pray tell?"

"To track the red devils. To rescue your niece."

"Believe me, Captain, saving dear Maria is uppermost on my mind," Gonzalez said. "But you heard Pvt. Batres. My brother and Capt. Filisola are hot on the heels of the Apaches. We would be duplicating their efforts, would we not, if we went to Adobe Wells? It would be a great waste of time." The colonel paused to flick a speck of dirt from his sleeve. "No, Captain, to rescue my niece we must think like the savages who stole her. We must answer certain questions. Where will they go now that they have her? Which route will they take to reach their destination?"

"Do you have the answers, sir?"

"Of course," Gonzalez said matter-of-factly. "Since we are dealing with renegades, we know they will make for either the Dragoon or the Chiricahua Mountains north of the border. And knowing Apaches as I do, I believe that they will take the most direct route."

"Which would be, sir?"

"North from Adobe Wells to Roca Pass. Over

the pass to the east slope, and then north to Caliente Springs. From there it is only a day's journey to the border and safety."

Mora was a highly competent officer. He had spent over an hour trying to deduce the route the Apaches would take. After carefully considering all the options, all the known trails and even those rarely used, he still had not been able to form a mental map of the course the renegades would follow. But the colonel laid it out as plainly as if he had been told by those they chased, and Capt. Mora knew his superior was right.

"You never cease to astound me, sir," Mora said. "How is it that you can think like Apaches? Are you part Chiricahua or Mescalero yourself?"

The colonel chuckled. "God forbid that I should have any red blood in my veins. I don't think like them, Captain. I outthink them. You too must learn to outwit your enemies if you ever hope to advance high in rank."

"I try, sir, but I have a long way to go before I will be as good as you are."

Col. Gonzalez liked it when his men flattered him, so long as the flattery was sincere and truthful. Grinning, he motioned, and his four captains drew alongside him. "Soon we will come to a parting of the ways. At the next junction we will split the command into four parts."

"Is it advisable to split our forces, sir?" Capt. Bonita asked.

"We are up against five Apaches, not five hundred," Gonzalez replied. "You, Bonita, will take forty men and head due west as far as Roca Pass. If you do not strike the Apaches' trail, you will head straight for Caliente Springs. That is where we will all regroup, come what may."

"As you wish, sir," Bonita said.

Gonzalez jabbed a finger at another captain. "You, Ortega, will swing twenty miles to the east in case I am wrong and the Apaches we are after are really Lipans who are making for Texas. Ride due north until you are east of Caliente Springs. If you strike their sign, you are to send men to notify me at once while you try to bring them to bay."

"Yes, Colonel."

"Capt. Hildago, you will take your patrol toward Agua Prieta. The same applies to you."

"Sir!"

"I will take the remaining men and strike out directly for Caliente Springs, with Capt. Mora as my adjutant. No matter what happens, gentlemen, I expect to see the command reunited within two days. Are there any questions?"

No one had any, but Mora did have a comment to make. "I see what you are doing, sir. You're launching a four-pronged pincer movement with the idea of catching the Apaches between two of the prongs."

"There's hope for you yet, Mora," Gonzalez said, and they all shared a chuckle. "In case that plan fails, I fully intend to reach Calienta Springs before they do and set up a suitable reception."

"We will have to push the men harder than we ever have before to get to the Springs in time," Capt. Mora said.

"We are going to ride straight through," Gonzalez said. "Spread the word among those who will go with us. And inform the packmaster that he must urge the pack animals on as swiftly as he can. I cannot afford to slacken my pace to suit his beasts of burden."

"Right away, Colonel."

"One more thing," Gonzalez said, and he slowed to give each of them a meaningful stare. "No matter which one of us stumbles on the Apaches first, one consideration is paramount. You must do whatever is necessary to save Maria. Do I make myself perfectly clear?"

The junior officers answered in the affirmative, and Capt. Mora went to turn his mount.

"Apparently I must elaborate," Gonzalez said curtly. He verified that none of the soldiers in the main column were close enough to overhear, then lowered his voice anyway. "These words are for your ears alone. In the event that one of us gets close enough to the Apaches to open fire on them, but not close enough to stop them, I expect whoever is in charge to do the right thing by my niece."

Mora and the other captains shared puzzled expressions. "Sir?" Mora said.

"You must not let the Apaches take her. No matter what."

"I'm not certain that I understand," Mora said.

"Are you deaf? If it appears to you that the Apaches are going to escape with Maria, you are to deprive them of their captive."

Again Mora and the rest exchanged looks, only this time they were much more grim. It was Mora who had the courage to speak the words uppermost on all their minds. "You can't be saying what we think you are saying, Colonel."

"Must I spell it out for you? If we are unable

to save her, we must spare her the ordeal of being a captive for the rest of her days." Eloquent appeal lit his eyes. "If you are left with no other option, put a bullet through her brain."

Chapter Eight

Clay Taggart lost the trail an hour before sunset. The wily bandits had been able to reach the Baked Plain, as the locals called it, a seemingly endless expanse of arid earth which had been baked rock hard by the scorching sun. The ground was so hard that men on foot left no tracks whatsoever, while men on horseback left tiny scratches and nicks if they left any sign at all.

Only the very best of trackers could trail anyone across the Baked Plain. And although Clay had learned enough about the craft from the Apaches to qualify him as competent, he wasn't as good as they were and he knew it.

Consequently, on reaching the plain, Clay was forced to scour every yard of ground carefully for the telltale signs so crucial to his finding Maria Gonzalez. Even as he sweated and toiled, losing precious time with every minute of delay, his

Bloodbath

conscience waged a tug-of-war with his common sense.

It was stupid of him to be going to all this trouble, Clay kept telling himself. Maria meant nothing to him. She was a captive, not a friend. He would be better off if he turned around, rejoined the Chiricahuas, and let her suffer the fate in store for her. What did it matter to him?

But Clay forged on anyway. He couldn't say why exactly. It was not as if he cared for her, not as if she meant anything to him. He preferred to think that he was going to so much trouble on her behalf simply because the bandits had gotten the better of him by whisking her away right out from under his very nose, and he did not like for anyone to get the better of him.

Then Clay lost the trail. He was several miles into the Baked Plain when the signs petered out. There were no more faint hoof marks, no more scratches to go by. He made a circuit of the immediate area and still found nothing. It was as if the bandits had vanished off the face of the planet.

But Clay knew better. He suspected that the bandits had thought to wrap the hooves of their mounts in strips cut from a blanket, leaving him with no idea which way the vermin were headed, and the sun was fast dipping toward the western horizon.

Clay had a decision to make. Should he do what was best and go back? Or should he try to outguess the bastards? Since the bandits had stuck to a straight easterly course since entering the Baked Plain, the logical conclusion was that they were still bearing due east.

But if that were the case, Clay reflected, why had they all of a sudden bothered to wrap the hooves of their horses? He figured it was because they had changed direction and didn't want possible pursuers to know the fact. If so, which way should he go?

West was out of the question. Clay had come from the west and would have seen them. By the same token, the northwest and southwest were not likely choices as both would take the bandits back toward the mountains and the Apaches. Since Clay doubted the bandits were still heading due east, that left him two directions to pick from: the southeast or the northeast.

Clay picked northeast. Miles to the southeast lay the presidio of Janos, and no bandit in his right mind would go anywhere near it. He put the horse into a distance-eating lope, watching the animal's shadow steadily lengthen as the sun sank steadily lower.

In due course darkness claimed the Baked Plain. Clay navigated by the stars, a trick he had learned long before he had met Delgadito. All a man had to do was locate the North Star, which was done by first locating the Big Dipper. The two stars that formed the side of the dipper farthest from the handle always pointed at the North Star.

Once the sun was gone, a cool breeze swept across the plain, bringing welcome relief. Clay stopped often to look and listen. The bandits might have stopped for the night and he didn't care to blunder into them.

It was almost midnight when Clay spied a flickering dot of light far ahead. He closed his eyes and rubbed them, then looked again to confirm his weary senses weren't playing a trick on him. The light was still there.

About the same time Clay noticed brush and weeds on either side of him. He had crossed the plain.

Circling to the south, Clay came up on the fire as stealthily as a mountain lion stalking prey. He dismounted and ground hitched the horse several hundred yards off so the animal wouldn't catch the scent of other horses and whinny to them.

Clay held the Winchester in his left hand as he padded through the brush, avoiding spots where twigs lay and trying not to step on brittle rocks that would crack and alert the bandits. He was some ways from the camp when their gruff laughter and lusty curses reached his ears. He did not hear Maria's voice.

Going faster, Clay was soon close enough to distinguish bulky shapes seated around the fire. He flattened and snaked to a cactus. Peeking past the spines, he counted five outlaws. The big, bearded leader was talking.

"We'll go to Monterrey next. I know a man there who would be all too happy to take Ramon's place. Those stinking Apaches!"

"Poor Ramon," another said. "Just this morning he was joking about the time we strangled that old prospector and the bastard's mule kicked me when I tried to open the packs on its back."

"I remember," a third man said. "We killed that worthless old fool for nothing. All he had on him were a few pesos and sacks of fool's gold."

"The desert scrambled his brains," a fourth said. "It does that, you know."

Clay shut out their banter and scanned the area. He saw their horses tethered in a row to the north of the fire. Saddles and packs had been deposited at random. Maria Gonzalez was nowhere to be seen, making Clay wonder if the cutthroats had already had their fun and disposed of her. Then his ears pricked up with interested.

"I hope it does not take us long to contact the Comanches," Vargas said. "With the gold we get for the girl, we will have a grand time in Monterrey."

"I can't wait to be in a city again," a lean bandit said. "I am going to buy a different whore every day the whole time we are there."

"You and your whores. One of these times a whore will leave you with a memento of her affection, and we will have to listen to you moan every time you take a leak."

Their rowdy laugher was Clay's cue to crawl closer. He had no cover, but it couldn't be helped. Holding his face low to the ground, he sought Maria in every shadow.

"Speaking of women," one of the cutthroats said, "what about the bitch? Comanches don't care if the merchandise is damaged a little. Why don't we all take turns?"

"I agree with Louis," the lean one said. "It has been weeks since we treated ourselves. How about it, Vargas?"

Clay recognized the name. Vargas's fame had spread north of the border after his gang waylaid a wagon train bound for Tucson and made off with every last valuable the pioneers possessed. Lawmen had chased Vargas to Mexico, but did not go beyond their jurisdiction.

Bloodbath

"I suppose we should," Vargas said. "To be fair, we will draw twigs. Whoever gets the short one wins the honor of tasting her nectar first, eh?"

"Who holds the twigs?" the lean one asked.

"I will."

By the looks the bandits gave their leader, it was clear they trusted him about as far as they could heave him. But such was the fear Vargas instilled in them that not one complained.

Clay watched Louis stand and walk to what appeared to be a pile of blankets and tack. Louis bent down to grab hold of something, and when the bandit straightened, the blankets uncoiled to reveal Maria Gonzalez. The firelight showed dried blood plastered to the right side of her head. Her hair was matted and slick. She moved awkwardly when Louis pushed her toward his companions.

"Move it, damn you," Louis grumbled.

Stumbling, Maria shuffled over and stood swaying near Vargas. Her clothes were in the same deplorable state as her head, coated with dirt and grime as well as being badly torn and wrinkled.

"Ah, my little flower," Vargas said sarcastically, "did you enjoy your nap?"

Maria gazed blankly at him. Like a striking serpent, Vargas swung, viciously smacking her across the cheek. Maria staggered, but did not go down. Her cheek was split, blood trickling to her chin.

"The next time I ask you a question, bitch," Vargas said, "you will answer me or I will knock out a few of your teeth to teach you better manners."

The bandits thought their leader was hilarious.

"Now did you enjoy your nap?" Vargas repeated.

"Yes."

The word was croaked, barely audible to Clay as he crept ever nearer.

"Excellent," the bandit leader said, taunting her. "We have decided that we want to be entertained tonight. Can you guess who will provide the entertainment?"

Maria marshaled the energy to spin and flee, but she hardly took two steps when Louis pounced and held her in place despite her feeble attempts to break loose.

Vargas winked at the others. "A man would think she was playing hard to get. Or maybe she is the shy type."

"Perhaps she is a virgin," another said.

Clay saw the wicked delight that came over the five of them. They were all so intent on their victim that he had been able to crawl within 15 feet of the fire and still not been spotted. He drew the rifle close to his chest and curled his thumb around the hammer. Soon, he would make his play.

"If only she was!" Vargas declared. "It has been ages since I had a virgin. They are getting harder to find the older I become."

"That is because the only women you bed anymore are whores," Louis said. "If a man wants a virgin, he must take up religion and attend church. Virgins like to kneel in pews, not sit in bars."

"Since when have you become such a philosopher?" Vargas asked.

"It is a fact of life," Louis insisted. "A woman

does not spend all her free time at a cantina if she wants to remain a virgin."

"Who cares?" the skinny one said. "Why are we doing all this talking when she's ripe for the plucking? Someone find twigs for us to use."

Clay had no forewarning. One of the bandits suddenly stood and came straight toward him, scouring the ground for twigs. In another few seconds the man would spot him. Under the circumstances there was only one thing he could do, and he did it.

Sweeping onto his knees, Clay centered the Winchester on the bandit's chest and stroked the trigger. The slug flung the man back and he crashed down on top of the fire, sending flames and a shower of sparkling embers in all directions. For several heartbeats the startled bandits sat there gaping.

Clay took prompt advantage of their reaction. Pivoting, he vented a war whoop while aiming at a second man; then he fired. The impact lifted the bandit clean off the ground and left him sprawled on his back with a red hole oozing gore in the middle of his forehead.

Belatedly, the bandits roused to life, all three palming pistols and blazing wildly away.

Bullets whizzed by overhead as Clay rose and ran to the right. He fired on the fly, working the lever smoothly. His shots thudded into a saddle vacated an instant before by Louis.

The bandits were scrambling toward their horses, shooting as they retreated, their shots poorly aimed.

Clay imagined that they thought there was more than one warrior. He lent credence to their

111

assumption by continuing to move in a circle and firing every few steps.

Vargas leaped up, knocking Maria aside. Endowed with the longest stride, he reached the string first. There he vaulted onto the biggest animal without missing a beat, tore at the tether rope, and wheeled into the night. He did not stay to help his friends.

A clear shot at Louis's back presented itself. Clay could no more pass it up than he could stop breathing. But as he fired, the third and last bandit cut around behind Louis to get to one of the horses. The slug shattered the man's spine and he fell to the dirt.

Meanwhile, Louis dashed around to the far side of a chestnut and swiftly swung astride the animal. He had the presence of mind to bend low as he turned the horse to flee in the wake of the bandit leader.

The Winchester lever made a rasping noise as Clay worked it forward and back. He tried to get a bead on either rider, but they were lost amidst the black veil of nocturnal gloom before he could shoot.

In baffled annoyance Clay jerked the rifle down. He made sure the hoofbeats receded into the distance before he darted to the young woman's side and lightly clasped her elbow. She stared at him without a glimmer of emotion.

"Maria, it's Clay. What did they do to you? How badly are you hurt?"

"Clay?" she said. On seeing his face she took a step back in terror and wailed. "You're the White Apache! You want to rape me, just like they did!"

Bloodbath

Again Clay had no warning. Maria flew into him with her nails hooked to claw out his eyes. It was all he could do to bring his arms up to protect himself. In her panic she screeched like a wildcat and kicked at his shins.

"Stop!" Clay shouted, but to no avail. He backed up under her onslaught, trying his utmost not to hurt her, but at the same time not willing to let her harm him. Her features were those of a person gone berserk. She didn't seem to care that he was heavily armed and the only weapons she had were her fingernails.

Clay felt a searing pain in his forearm. He knew that he couldn't hold her at bay much longer. For her own sake he had to stop her, and with that end in mind he gripped the Winchester in both hands in preparation for ramming the stock into her stomach. To his consternation, Maria abruptly halted, gave a little cry, and keeled over.

Vargas was certain that a dozen savages had swooped down on his band. He raced blindly on into the moonless night, whipping his reins and using the rowels on his large spurs to their full advantage. Unlike American cowboys who filed the sharp points of their rowels down in order not to hurt their animals, Vargas had used a file to sharpen his. When he applied his spurs, the horse knew it.

Soon Vargas became aware that someone was after him. He glanced over his shoulder and spied a dim figure galloping a score of yards behind him.

An Apache! Vargas thought. He was not about to let the red demon carve his heart out. Pointing

113

his pistol, he tried to aim but it was impossible to hold the six-gun steady. He fired anyway, thinking he might at least make the Apache break off the pursuit.

"Vargas! It's Louis! For God's sake, don't shoot!"

Most men would have been embarrassed by the mistake, but not Vargas. "Why the hell didn't you let me know sooner? "I could have killed you!" He slowed to allow Louis to catch up. "Is there no one else? What about Alfredo?"

"Shot dead near the horses."

"Damn those Apache bastards all to hell!" Vargas raged.

"Maybe you should not yell so loud," Louis said. "They might still be after us."

The reminder scared Vargas into knuckling down to a long, hard ride. Neither of them spoke again until, five miles later, they stopped on top of a small knoll to give their horses a breather.

"I don't see any sign of them," Louis said.

"Idiot. Haven't you learned anything?" Vargas said. "A man never sees Apaches until it is too late. Look at what just happened. We were nearly wiped out before we knew what hit us by fifteen or twenty of those sons of bitches."

Louis gave a little cough. "I don't think there were quite that many, amigo."

"How many then?"

"One."

Vargas did not suffer fools gladly. He gave the smaller man the sort of look that had caused many a fool to cringe, but Louis refused to be intimidated.

"Think about it. Count the number of shots that

were fired. I would say it was one warrior with a rifle."

"You're loco," Vargas said. Yet when he reviewed the attack, he had to admit that there might well have been a lone attacker. The insight flushed him with pulsating rage. He disliked being made a fool of even more than he disliked fools.

"So where do we go from here?" Louis said. "Monterrey or another city? We need to find three or four good men now, not just one."

"First we need to get the bitch back."

Louis's neck had a way of cracking like a whip when he snapped his head around. "You have a poor sense of humor."

"Who's joking? If there's only one Apache, as you believe, then it shouldn't be too hard for us to hunt him down and pay him back for all the grief he has caused us," Vargas said. "And must I remind you that now more than ever we need whatever the Comanches will give us for the girl?"

"But this is an Apache we're talking about. Who cares if there is just one? He killed three of us in twice as many seconds. Let him have the girl and good riddance."

"I am going to get her back." Vargas refused to change his mind. Once he came to a decision, he stuck to it as tenaciously as glue. "You can come or you can ride off and hear about your cowardice in every cantina between here and the border."

"You wouldn't."

Vargas rode to the bottom of the knoll without answering. Humiliation was sometimes as potent as fear in persuading others to do something against their will.

In a minute Vargas heard the sound of Louis's horse as it overtook his. He pretended not to notice and refrained from smiling smugly so as not to antagonize Louis. The truth was, Vargas needed to have Louis along. He had small hope of slaying the Apache on his own.

"You are going back there right this minute?" the other bandito asked.

"Yes."

"Can't it wait until morning?"

"Think about it," Vargas said. "He thinks that he has driven us off. The last thing he would expect is for us to return before daybreak. With the bitch hurt, he might even stay at our camp until first light. We cannot let the chance go by."

"I hope you know what you are doing."

"Don't I always?" Vargas said, although both of them were fully aware his long string of successful robberies, murders, and raids was due more to an incredible run of luck than to any genius on his part.

The jeopardy into which they were placing themselves made both men somber. They held their mounts to a brisk walk, slowing when Vargas figured they had less than a mile to go. Among a stand of mesquite they finally halted and dismounted.

"It is not too late to change our minds," Louis said.

"You can stay here with the horses if you want," Vargas said scornfully, although inwardly he hoped Louis would do no such thing. Hunkering down, he removed his spurs and placed them in his saddlebags for safekeeping. He looked at

Louis and was glad to see his example being followed.

In the distance, gleaming palely, was the campfire. Vargas headed toward it, hunched low, trying to move quietly. He stopped frequently. Deep within him a tiny voice screamed that he should turn around and give up his insane notion before he paid for his stupidity with his life. But he had always been a proud man and he was not about to shame himself by turning yellow at the last minute. This unexpected bravery surprised him immensely. He was at a loss to explain it.

A gulch 200 yards from the camp gave Vargas a spot to lie low while the fire did the same. He sought signs of the Apache and the woman, and he thought he saw one of them moving about. That would be the savage, he reasoned.

Louis said nothing and did nothing but stare bleakly off into the darkness as if his certain death was imminent. He started when Vargas touched him and motioned for them to go on.

Vargas fed a round into the chamber of his rifle. Slipping from bush to bush, he closed on his prey. He expected to hear the crash of a gun but apparently the Apache believed himself to be safe. It was a fatal mistake, Vargas thought.

The bandito leader and Louis knelt behind a wide bush 30 feet from where their friends lay in the dust. Vargas took a deep breath, nodded at Louis, reared upright, and charged.

In concert, they aimed their rifles. In concert, they opened fire, shooting as rapidly as they could, emptying their weapons as they closed.

Nothing could have survived their volley of hot lead.

And nothing did.

Chapter Nine

"We should have gone with him," Cuchillo Negro said. When none of his fellow Chiricahuas responded to his statement, he said it again, adding, "He has stood by us through our hard times. We should stand by him."

The band had stopped for a rest at a small tank only Apaches knew about. It resembled a stone cistern and was halfway up the slope of a boulder-strewn hill situated in the middle of a parched stretch of landscape.

Fiero had just finished drinking. He made the sort of a sound a buffalo might make while cavorting in a wallow, then said, "I do not understand this strange concern of yours. So what if he has helped us? We have helped him. We owe him nothing."

"And he is a grown man, not a boy," Ponce said. "Men live or die by their own decisions, and it was his decision to go after the bandits."

None of the other warriors saw fit to comment on the fact that the youngest of them, whose claim to full manhood could be measured in moons instead of winters, was lecturing them on the nature of being a man.

Delgadito spoke next. "We have long prided ourselves on being able to do as we want when we want. We answer to no one but ourselves. Whether in times of peace or war, a warrior can walk the path that he sees fit to walk."

"That is part of our problem," Cuchillo Negro said.

Now the others all looked at him, and Fiero asked, "Since when is being free to do as one pleases a problem?"

"When it results in an entire people being conquered by another," Cuchillo Negro said. "Look at what happened to our people in our war with the white-eyes. They were able to beat us in our own land, in the mountains and deserts we have claimed as ours for more winters than anyone can remember. And why? Did they know our own land better than we did? No. Are the white-eyes better fighters than we are? No. They beat us because they have learned how to live and fight together, to put all their minds to one purpose and to see that purpose through to the end. That is the secret of the white-eyes. That is why they have been able to beat everyone who opposes them."

No one else commented. Secretly, they were all surprised. None of them had ever heard Cuchillo Negro say so much at one time. And he wasn't done.

"We have leaders, yes, but we do not make their will our will in all respects. As Fiero is so proud of pointing out, we do as we please. We go every which way. And because we do not know how to work together, we were weaker than the whites. It is not right to say that they shamed us by beating us. We shamed ourselves because our own weakness beat us."

"What would you have us do?" Fiero asked. "Become like the whites-eyes?"

"Yes."

"The heat has affected your brain," Ponce said.

"Because I want to see our people shake off the shackles of the Americans and go on living as we have always lived?" Cuchillo Negro said. "I tell you here and now that unless we learn to mold our wills to a single cause, as the white-eyes do, our people will never know true freedom again."

At this Delgadito's eyes narrowed. "So this is why you watch over Lickoyee-shis-inday like a mother dog over a pup. You hope he will teach us the secret of being of one mind in all things so that we can turn the white-eyes's strength against them and reclaim our land as our own?"

"A wise man learns from his enemies as well as his friends," Cuchillo Negro said.

Fiero uttered his customary snort. "We do not need to think like whites to defeat them. They conquered us because they have more men and more guns. All we need to rise up against them are more warriors who think as we do and more guns. It's as simple as that."

Cuchillo Negro rose and stepped into the sunlight. He knew it would be a waste of his time to argue the point with the firebrand, and he doubted very much that Ponce would come around to his way of thinking either. But he had hoped Delgadito would agree since, of them all, Delgadito was the deepest thinker. Maybe Delgadito did, he mused, but was unwilling to admit it.

As the warrior idly surveyed the horizon he glimpsed a pinpoint flash of light, then another and another until there were dozens, like stars sparkling low in the daytime sky. Only Cuchillo Negro knew better. At a low call from him, the others came into the open.

"*Nakai-yes*," Delgadito said. "Soldiers. Many soldiers."

"They must be after us," Ponce said.

"If so, they will never catch us," Fiero said. "The day I cannot elude a whole army of Mexicans is the day I take up basket weaving."

Delgadito had been studying the position of the pinpoints. "It is not our trail they follow," he said. "They are too far to the east."

"It does not matter," Cuchillo Negro said. "They are coming straight toward this hill. We must not be here when they arrive."

"So what if we are?" Fiero said. "The *Nakai-yes* have the senses of rocks. They will never spot us."

"But their horses might pick up our scent," Cuchillo Negro said. "And the four of us would be no match for as many soldiers as there appear to be. I, for one, do not intend to throw my life away needlessly."

Hefting his Winchester, Cuchillo Negro jogged to the bottom of the hill and swung to the northwest. They would be at Caliente Springs by morning; there they would rest up during the day. If Clay did not show by sunrise, the others would want to press on across the border. And he knew of no way to dissuade them.

Clay had better show up on time or he would find himself on his own.

The gurgle of rippling water brought Maria Gonzalez back to consciousness. She lay still, trying to recall where she was and what she had been doing last.

In a rush of harrowing memories, Maria remembered being taken captive by Apaches, fleeing with the bandits, trying to escape, and being hit by Vargas. She also recollected the attack on the camp and confronting the White Apache. Then what had happened?

"You can open your eyes if you wish. I have coffee ready."

Maria realized that there was indeed a strong scent of boiling brew in the air. The delicious odor made her stomach growl and her mouth water. She opened her eyes and saw the White Apache seated across a small fire from her, his elbows propped on his knees.

"I treated your wound with a poultice."

Reaching up, Maria found a crude compress on her head. She probed with her fingertips, assuring herself that she wasn't bleeding any longer. Encouraged, she went to sit up but was overcome by a wave of dizziness, not to mention intense pain in her back and her temple.

"I'd take it easy if I were you," Clay said. "You've been out for the most of the day but I doubt you're well enough yet to travel."

"Half the day?" Maria said. A glance to the west

confirmed the time. It also showed that they were in the shade afforded by a grove of cottonwoods on the bank of a narrow, shallow river. "Where are we? What happened to your four friends? And what do you plan to do with me now?"

Clay leaned back and arched an eyebrow at her. "You're welcome."

"What?"

"Where I hail from, it's polite to thank folks who have pulled your fat out of the fire. If I hadn't come along when I did, those bandits would have had their way with you and sold you to Comanches."

It would never have occurred to Maria that a man reputed to be a bloodthirsty renegade could have his feelings hurt by a failure to show proper gratitude, but that was the impression she had. "My apologies," she said stiffly. "I do thank you for what you've done, but I can't help but suspect you had an ulterior motive. You want me for yourself."

Clay bent forward to pour coffee into a battered tin cup he had found in the saddlebags of the bandit who had tried to bushwhack him. "I stole you from your parents. That makes you my responsibility."

"I thought as much," Maria said in contempt. "You did not go to so much trouble on my behalf."

"As for your questions," Clay said, "we're camped next to the Rio de Bavisque. My four friends, as you call them, wanted nothing more to do with you. And my plan is the same as it's always been. I aim to take you to Arizona Territory."

Bloodbath

Maria closed her eyes, despondent. It seemed her grueling ordeal would never end. She was losing hope that she would ever see her mother and father again. Twisting her head, she looked down at herself and felt tears well up. Her clothes were in the worst shape of any clothing she had ever worn, and she was no better off. Dust clung to her from head to toe. Dried blood clotted her hair and stuck to her tattered dress. She was in dire need of a bath. If she had the choice, she would have given anything to be back on the family hacienda attended by her devoted servants.

Clay Taggart noticed the senorita's sadness, but did not let on. Regret came over him, regret which he promptly shrugged off. He had no business feeling sorry for her. A true Apache wouldn't, and he was trying to pattern his behavior and attitudes after those of his Chiricahua pards.

He carried the cup around the fire and handed it to her without saying a word. Her eyes lingered on him as he took his seat.

"May I ask you a question?" Maria asked.

"I'd be surprised if you didn't."

Cradling the cup gingerly, Maria took a few short sips and sighed as the hot brew washed down her throat. "I would very much like to know why you are the way you are. Once you mentioned getting revenge on someone who had wronged you. Does it have something to do with why you have taken up with Apaches?"

"You want my life's story, in other words," Clay said dryly. "Sorry, ma'am. I happen to believe that a man's past is his own business and no one else's. If you're digging for something that would get me to change my mind about you, you're plumb out of luck."

"It must be nice to know everything," Maria said, acid in her voice.

"I wouldn't last very long if I was an idiot," Clay said, leaning on an elbow and taking a sip from another cup. It had been a while since last he had enjoyed coffee and he had forgotten how well it hit the spot after a long day in the saddle.

"I would guess you have a lot of hatred pent up inside of you," Maria said.

"Why? Because I kidnapped lovely women?"

"Because you will let no one get close to you except your Apache friends. It is as if you have built a wall around yourself so that none can see into your soul."

Clay said nothing. He had to hand it to her though. For such a young filly, she was terribly shrewd—and desperate. She would do anything to keep from being taken across the border, and he made a mental note to watch her closely from then on out.

Weakness put a stop to Maria's chatter. She finished half the cup, then set it aside and lay back down. She needed her wits more than ever, and they were denied her by the severe loss of blood she had suffered. A good night's sleep would restore some of her strength but it was too early to doze off and she did not want to anyway.

Horses nickered nearby. Maria turned her head and saw three tied to cottonwoods. She toyed with the idea of sneaking to them after dark, but doubted her nerves would be equal to the occasion.

As if the White Apache could read her mind, he said, "Don't be getting any silly notions, senorita. We're miles from nowhere and it would be easy as pie for me to catch you again."

Clay slowly polished off the cup and refilled it. Coffee was a luxury he wasn't about to pass up. The Chirichuas had little use for it. They'd drink it on occasion, but they weren't addicted, like most whites. Delgadito's bunch even refrained from mescal and tizwin, hard drinks most Apaches favored.

As Clay drank, he thanked Lady Luck for smiling on him back at the bandito camp. He had intended to stay there the whole night through, but then had taken to thinking about the pair who slipped away. It wouldn't have been at all out of character for the murderous twosome to circle around and shoot him. So he had saddled three horses, loaded as many supplies as he could onto one, draped the woman over another, and ridden off.

He hadn't traveled more than a quarter of a mile when the night had rocked to rifle fire. The bandits had done just as he'd figured they would. He'd grinned, wishing he could have heard their lusty curses when they had aired their lungs over his absence.

Clay had given the bandits the slip, and he could relax until he was reunited with Delgadito. Well, not relax entirely, he mused, since he was in a region where bandits were as numerous as fleas on an old hound dog. Plus there was the threat of scalphunters, scum paid by the Sonoran government to exterminate any Apache caught south of the border. They earned their bounty by showing Apache scalps as proof of their performance. And the government didn't care if the scalps were those of warriors, women, or children. So long as they were Indian scalps, the scalphunters received their blood money.

Which had created a new problem in itself. Scalphunters were not notorious for being the most scrupulous of men. When Apaches were scarce, they took to killing any Indians they could find. Friendly tribes such as the Pimas and Maricopas lost many of their number who went off to hunt or fetch water or gather roots and were never seen again. It took a while for the friendly tribes to put two and two together, and henceforth they never went anywhere except in numbers sufficient to deter the greedy scalphunters.

A faint sound brought Clay's reverie to an end. It was so faint that for a full ten seconds he wondered if he had really heard the dull thud of a hoof. Then he heard another and knew someone was sneaking up on their campsite from the southeast.

Rolling to his feet with the Winchester in hand, Clay peered through the cottonwoods and spied several riders approaching. He had been careless! He had gone and built the fire too big, a mistake no true Apache would ever make. The column of smoke was probably visible for miles.

Clay had to think fast. There was no time to put out the fire, hide the charred limbs, load up the gear, and get the hell out of there.

Maria, he saw, had fallen asleep. He took a step closer to awaken her, but changed his mind. It might have been a blessing in disguise.

Bloodbath

Quickly Clay melted into the cottonwoods and knelt in a clump of brush. The four riders were close enough to note details. Their dusty uniforms revealed they were soldiers. Since there were too few to constitute a patrol, Clay deduced they had been sent on ahead of a large column.

As Clay watched the troopers warily approach the camp, he studied them as would an Apache, noting which one was the most alert, which appeared the most dangerous, which would be the easiest to slay. He stopped thinking like a white rancher and instead thought like a Chiricahua warrior.

When the patrol drew rein a few dozen feet from Maria, it was not Clay Taggart, rancher, who raised a rifle to his shoulder, but Lickoyee-shis-inday, Apache.

A corporal led the patrol. He had spotted Maria, and it was clear that he did not know what to make of the situation. To find a woman sleeping peacefully by herself in the middle of nowhere was not a common occurrence.

The corporal whispered orders. All four soldiers dismounted. Fanning out, they converged on the camp, moving slowly, raking the undergrowth for evidence of hostiles.

Clay let them come nearer. He was so well hidden that they would have to be right on top of the bush to notice him and he was not going to let them get that close. Since the corporal was the one the others would rely on in a crisis, he targeted the corporal first, centering the sights squarely on the man's torso.

But as so often happened in life, the unexpected reared its head in the shapely form of Maria

Gonzalez, who choose that particular moment to snap out of her slumber. Whether she heard or sensed the soldiers, she sat bolt upright, and on seeing them she screeched in Spanish, "Look out! The White Apache is here!"

The corporal dropped into a crouch just as Clay applied pressure to the trigger and the bullet took off the man's hat instead of his head.

The bush hid the muzzle flash but the four soldiers had a good idea of where the shot had come from and they cut loose with military precision.

Slugs zipped past Clay, clipping the bush, nicking an arm. He tracked the corporal as the man rose and ran to Maria. She started to rise, her hand reaching for the corporal's. Clay drilled the man as their fingers touched.

Maria's scream rivaled the din of the gunfire.

Shifting, Clay shot a second trooper. The last two elected to preserve their lives and sprinted toward their horses. Clay elevated the Winchester.

To a Chiricahua, horses were animals. No more, no less. They were not viewed as pets, never regarded with affection. More often than not, horses were eaten. Every boy knew that to become attached to one was the height of folly.

Clay Taggart had been reared differently. As a rancher, he had ridden horses daily and worked with them from dawn until dusk. There had been several he had liked immensely.

But since he had joined with the Apache, Clay had learned to harbor no such sentiments. Horses were horses, and in this instance, when they were the means his enemies would use to bring even more enemies, they had to be dealt

130

with accordingly. In rapid order he dropped three of them with slugs through the head. The fourth, however, heard its fellows whinny as they fell, and it fled.

The two soldiers were left stranded. One darted in among the trees. The other whirled and fired at random, a man whose reason had been replaced by riveting fear.

Working the lever, Clay aimed and fired. He had such confidence in his marksmanship that he didn't wait to see if the man went down, but leaped to his feet and raced after the soldier who had fled.

Crashing in the growth ahead told Clay which direction to take. Like a black-tailed buck he bounded through the cottonwoods at a speed no white man or Mexican could equal. But the soldier was fleeing for his life, and fright was known to lend strength and speed to ordinary limbs. It took over a minute of hard running before Clay spied his quarry. The soldier also spied him.

Clay had to throw himself to the ground as the trooper's carbine cracked. Flipping to the right, he rose and went to fire but the man had already whirled and run off. Too many trees were between them.

Swinging to the north, Clay pumped his legs, taking a course parallel to that of the soldier. He had gone over 50 feet when he realized the cottonwoods had fallen completely silent. Instantly he stopped and crouched.

The soldier was crafty. He had gone to ground in the hope of flushing the White Apache out.

It wouldn't be that easy, Clay reflected as he

stalked to a tree with low limbs. Climbing ten feet, he paused. From there he had a bird's-eye view of the area where he had last seen the trooper. The man lay in high grass, facing toward the camp, the carbine tucked to his shoulder.

Clay braced the barrel of his Winchester against the trunk, held the bead steady for a three count, and fired. The slug penetrated the rear of the soldier's head and exploded out from his forehead in a rain of flesh and brains.

Jumping down, Clay made for the camp. He didn't know how close the main column was and had to consider the likelihood that the shots had been heard. It was imperative he get the woman out of there.

There was only one problem.

When Clay emerged from the vegetation at the edge of clearing, he discovered that Maria Gonzalez was gone.

Chapter Ten

Their camp had been established for the night. The horses had been tethered and perimeter sentries posted.

Col. Jose Gonzalez and Capt. Mora were seated by one of several fires, drinking coffee and discussing the route they would take the next day, when one of the sentries yelled that a horse was fast approaching. Moments later a riderless horse burst into the encampment and halted, its sides heaving.

Soldiers leaped to their feet, carbines at the ready. The colonel and his aide rushed to the horse and Capt. Mora seized the reins. But there was little chance of the animal running off. It was too exhausted to lift a leg.

"This is one of ours," Mora said, smacking the regulation-issue saddle. "But whose?"

"I recognize the blaze on its chest," Col. Gonzalez said. "This is the mount issued to

Cpl. Hildago. He was sent ahead to see how close we are to the Rio de Bavisque. He must have been ambushed, either by bandits or the Apaches we are after." Spinning, the colonel rasped out orders. "Break camp immediately! Douse those fires! I want every man mounted and ready to ride in five minutes."

A flurry of activity ensued as every man rushed to obey. Unlike lazier commanders, who were content to spend all their time behind their desk while their men languished in barracks, Col. Gonzalez drilled his troops daily. There was no more efficient unit in all of Mexico, which the men proved by being in the saddle in the time stipulated.

Col. Gonzalez swung into the leather, rose in the stirrups, and whipped his arm forward. Capt. Mora issued the order to move out, and 40 horses were rapidly brought to a canter.

They wound northward along a dusty ribbon. Mora stared at the inky sky and said, "Would it not have been advisable to have waited until morning, Colonel? We can not see a thing in this soup."

"The missing troopers are all that matter. Some of them might still be alive," Gonzalez answered. "Always put the welfare of your men above all other considerations, Captain. It is the earmark of a genuine leader."

"I wholeheartedly agree, sir. But how will we locate them if we cannot track them?"

"We will trust in Providence. If nothing else, even if we do not find any trace of them, we will have done our duty. Our men will respect us for that. And never forget that earning the respect

Bloodbath

of those you command is the first step toward earning their loyalty."

From then on, they knuckled down to the business of riding. In due time they bore to the northwest. It was over two hours later that a band of trees materialized in the distance. And where there were trees, Capt. Mora knew, there was usually water.

"The river," he said.

"Look," Col. Gonzalez said, pointing.

A mile or more away glittered a yellowish-orange finger of flame.

"We have them!" Mora said.

At that very moment other eyes were on the same fire. Martin Gonzalez reined up on a ridge to the west and pushed his sombrero back on his head. "Could it be? Would they be careless enough to make a fire with us on their trail?"

"Maybe they think that we have given up," Capt. Filisola said. "Or it might not be them at all."

"Maybe we should send Pedro and Sgt. Amat on ahead to scout out the situation," Martin said. "We don't want to ride into a trap."

"It's best if we all stick together," Filisola said. "If it is the Apaches, with a little luck we can surround them. And for that we'll need every man we have." He assumed the lead and carefully picked his way downward. Truth to tell, he was elated by the sight of that distant camp. It inspired his flagging hope. As hour after hour had gone by with no sign of the savages or their captive, he'd had to confront the very real prospect that he would never set eyes on the lovely senorita again. A pall of gloom had seized his soul and refused to let go.

135

Now, Capt. Filisola felt like a man reborn. Perhaps there was a prayer after all. Perhaps he would get to have the wonderful pleasure of Maria Gonzalez's company, not once but many times. And if she wound up being as enamored of him as he was of her, well, who was to say what might happen?

Filisola grinned. Maybe it was time he gave serious thought to giving up the bachelor life. His looks and charm would not last forever. And there were much worse fates than marrying into one of the richest families in Mexico.

Martin Gonzalez was equally elated. He had about given his precious daughter up as lost to him forever, a calamity he did not know if he could endure.

Martin often thought of a friend whose own daughter had been abducted. Later the friend had learned that she had been made the wife of a notorious Apache. Through intermediaries, the friend had tired to buy her, but the Apache refused. The friend had offered to trade for her, to give as many guns and horses and whatever else the Apache might want. Still the Apache declined.

In despair the poor father had put the barrel of a cocked pistol in his mouth and pulled the trigger. The very next day a messenger had arrived, sent by the warrior to say that he had changed his mind and was willing to trade. When the Apache found out the father had killed himself, the warrior slew the daughter because he did not want a wife who came from a bloodline of weaklings.

Many times since Maria had been taken, Martin

wondered how well he would hold up if he failed to save her. His grief might tempt him to commit the same act as his friend. But he couldn't. Theresa would need him more than ever.

Capt. Filisola swung to the northwest to approach the fire through the cottonwoods. He had the men dismount and advance in skirmish order. They had gone 50 yards when he realized the camp was on the other side of the Rio de Bavisque.

Meanwhile, Col. Jose Gonzalez led his own men in a skirmish line from the southeast. He strode at the center of the line, his pistol in one hand, his saber in the other. The fire, he saw, had burned low. Near it, he could just make out the outlines of men asleep.

The colonel whispered an order to Capt. Mora, which was relayed down the line in both directions. The ends turned inward, making a horseshoe formation, which resulted in the camp being ringed on three sides. Advancing silently, their every nerve on edge, the troopers closed in on their age-old enemies.

On the north bank, Sgt. Amat turned to Capt. Filisola and whispered, "I see men moving in the dark beyond the camp, sir. Many men."

Filisola squinted and saw figures creeping toward the river. It excited him. His racing mind hit on the obvious conclusion: the White Apache and those with him had joined up with a larger band of renegades, and the savages knew that a small party was trying to sneak up on them.

"Who are they?" Martin Gonzalez asked. "What do we do?"

Before Filisola could answer, one of the nervous troopers in his patrol spotted the figures, jumped to the same conclusion he had, and did what any other man might have done under the same circumstances. Without thinking, the trooper aimed his carbine and fired. His shot inadvertently served as the signal for all the soldiers and vaqueros on the north bank to open fire. Few had clear targets but they fired anyway. When dealing with Apaches, every man there had learned long ago that those who lived longest were those quickest on the trigger.

The initial volley tore into the soldiers moving toward the dwindling fire. Col. Gonzalez and his men were concentrating on the prone forms near it. The first inkling they had that there was anyone else within ten miles of the spot came when slugs tore through the air around them. Two troopers fell, one howling in agony at the burning lead in his gut.

Col. Gonzalez reacted as would any seasoned commander. He saw the muzzle flashes on the other side of the Rio de Bavisque and bellowed, "More Apaches! Fire at will!" Then he proceeded to blast away with his pistol.

All along the line, soldiers crouched or knelt and shot round after round at the north bank while those on the north bank did the same at the south bank.

Men fell on both sides. Here a trooper toppled over, screaming. There a vaquero went down, cursing Apaches with his drying breath.

It soon became apparent to Capt. Filisola that he was greatly outnumbered. He rose to order a retreat and felt a searing pang in his right shoulder. The impact spun him around, and in the act of spinning, his left boot caught in the bush he had been behind. His leg started to sweep out from under him. Frantically the captain tried to right himself but all he succeeded in doing was throwing himself more off balance, and the next thing he knew, he was tumbling down the bank to the water's edge.

Filisola heard bullets thud into the earth beside him. He was completely exposed and lying there helpless in the open. Propping his hands under him, he scrambled for cover.

On the south bank, Col. Gonzalez had seen a figure spill from the undergrowth. He couldn't credit the testimony of his own eyes when he saw that it was someone in uniform. For a few moments he thought it might be an Apache. Then the figure glanced toward the south side of the river, and despite the distance and the dark he knew immediately who it was.

Striding into the clearing, Col. Gonzalez raised his saber on high and thundered in the voice that could be heard by everyone, "Cease firing! Cease firing this moment, idiots! Cease firing!"

Capt. Filisola, in the act of clawing up the bank, froze, too stupefied to speak. The awful truth dawned and he wanted to burrow into the ground and cover himself with a ton of dirt so no one would ever find him.

The sight of the colonel shocked both sides into lowering their weapons. Martin ran down into the river and stood in the shallows, gaping. "Brother! I am so sorry! We thought that you and your men were Apaches."

"The same applies to us," Col. Gonzalez called

out. "Come across and we will tend the wounded." He turned to issue directions to his own men and noticed the forms that he had assumed were slumbering Apaches. To his consternation, they were dead soldiers, members of the patrol sent out with Cpl. Hildago.

Others were soon arranged in rows beside them. The battle had resulted in the deaths of four men, one of them a vaquero, and the wounding of seven others. Most of the wounds were minor.

Capt. Filisola sat glumly while his shoulder was being bandaged. He was convinced that his military career was at an end. The colonel was bound to report the incident. Filisola wouldn't be surprised if a military tribunal was called and he found himself on trial. Given the nature of his offense—firing on his superior officer—he'd be lucky if he got off easy with a life sentence.

Suddenly the moment Filisola dreaded was upon him. The colonel walked over and shooed all those within earshot away. "How bad is it?"

"I lost very little blood, sir," Filisola said. "In three weeks I should be as good as new."

The colonel sat down on the same log. "Well," he said softly, "we sure made a mess of things, didn't we? This is the first blemish on my record. I wouldn't be surprised if I'm recalled to Mexico City to answer an official inquiry."

"I will be right there with you," Capt. Filisola said. Impulsively, he gripped his superior's arm. "Please forgive my stupidity, Colonel. I should have stopped my men from firing until I had determined who we were shooting at."

"I made the same blunder," Col. Gonzalez said.

Bloodbath

"And while we were justified to a degree by the circumstances, those fat generals in Mexico City who have never served a day in the field can hardly be expected to appreciate the position we were in."

"True, unfortunately, sir," Filisola said, more depressed than ever.

"So perhaps it is best if they never have to sit in judgment on us," Col. Gonzalez said quietly.

"What are you saying?"

"Since we thought we were fighting Apaches, that is how our reports should read," the colonel said. "We came on an Apache camp we presumed to be deserted and were ambushed."

It would not have shocked Vicente Filisola more had the Pope decreed that the Bible was nothing more than a collection of old fables. "You are saying we should lie, sir?" he asked in a stunned whisper.

"I'm saying that sometimes a soldier must do that which is most expedient, not only on the field of battle, but in dealing with those higher in rank who are not in a position to understand the underlying facts of a particular case."

"Yes, sir," Filisola said, not entirely convinced. A lie by any other name was still a lie in his book.

Col. Gonzalez was a shrewd judge of men. He would not have risen so far if he were not. "What would you have us do, my good Captain? Ruin both of our careers over a mutual blunder? Our duty is first and foremost to our country and the people of Mexico, but would either be served by the scandal that would result? No, on all counts. It would be a shame for you to have your head put on the public chopping block so soon after your promotion." Sighing, the colonel rose and went to leave.

"What promotion?" Filisola asked.

"Didn't I tell you?" Col. Gonzalez said casually. "For being clever enough to figure out that the Apaches were going to attack my brother's party and the courage you displayed in rushing to his aid, I decided a promotion was in order. Before leaving the fort, I sent a dispatch to Hermosillo. In it, I informed them that you were the recipient of a field promotion to the rank of major." He stretched, then took another stride.

"Colonel," Filisola said, overcome with gratitude.

"Yes, Major?"

"I agree that it would ill serve our country for us to be punished for a simple mistake. But what about the men, sir? They will tell stories—"

"Show me a man with any brains who will stand on a rooftop and shout to the world that he is an idiot," Col. Gonzalez said. "As far as we are concerned, the only ears that matter are those in Mexico City. And in my capacity as Commander, I can guarantee that the only reports that will cross their desks are those we submit and that which Maj. Mora is required to file. But you need not worry about him. We just had a talk, and he is as pleased with his new promotion as you are. Trust me. I have been at this much longer than you have."

"I trust you with my life, Colonel."

Col. Gonzalez smiled and walked off. A little adroit maneuvering and he had turned a potential disaster into two promotions and added to his sterling record. The account he planned to submit would make it clear that were it not for his brilliance, the Apaches would have overwhelmed his unit.

The colonel thought of the shocked look on the captain's face at the suggestion they should lie. That was always the way with the young ones. They were too idealistic for their own good. They had yet to learn that, in the dog-eat-dog world into which they had been born, the biggest bones went to those dogs willing to fight for what was theirs.

And Col. Jose Gonzalez was too fond of being at the head of the pack to settle for anything less.

Half a mile to the east, four stocky, bronzed figures stood under the starlit sky waiting to see if the gunfire would resume.

"We must investigate," Cuchillo Negro said. "Clay might need our help."

"He can take care of himself," Ponce said.

They had been traveling fast and hard ever since they had spotted the soldiers earlier. So it had come as a considerable surprise when the sounds of the battle had risen to their ears—sounds that told them more soldiers were to the west of their position.

"This country crawls with *Nakai-yes*," Delgadito said. "If it is not bandits we run into, it is soldiers. The longer we remain, the bigger the risk we run."

"Risks are the spice of life," Fiero said. "For once I agree with Cuchillo Negro. We should go see what all the shooting was about. Even if Lickoyee-shis-inday is not involved, there might be Mexicans to kill, plunder to take."

"You never can turn your back on a good fight," Delgadito said. "And I was only mentioning the risk, not using it as an excuse to keep from doing what must be done. We will go."

Spreading out, the quartet flowed over the ground like living wraiths, making no more noise than the passage of the wind itself. In practically no time they were among cottonwoods, and they slowed down to get their bearings. Through the trees came the murmur of many men and the sound of many horses.

Fiero, as was his habit, moved into the lead. When battle loomed, he liked to be first into the fray. From cover to cover he flitted until he saw several fires and dozens of soldiers moving about, engaged in various tasks.

For more years than either side could remember, Apaches and Mexicans had despised one another. The Mexicans claimed it was because Apaches were bloodthirsty demons who thrived on war, which was true to a degree. The Apaches claimed it was because the Mexican government had continued the Spanish practice of enslaving Apaches to work in mines and killing them for bounty. Neither had any compunctions about killing the other.

So as Fiero sank onto his stomach and made like an eel, he had one idea uppermost on his mind: How many Mexicans could he slay and still get away?

Cuchillo Negro was only interested in learning whether Clay was safe. He rated Lickoyee-shisinday as invaluable to the Chiricahuas and did not want anything to happen to him.

Bloodbath

Delgadito was also concerned but his reason was not the same. He needed Clay Taggart to help rebuild his band so that one day he could again rise to a position of leadership.

Of the four, only Ponce saw no sense in the peril they were courting. The Apache creed was to kill without being killed, and to that end, warriors went to extraordinary lengths when going into battle to make sure there was always a means of retreat if the worst should happen. In this instance, though, they weren't bothering to scout the area, to check all the avenues of approach, to assess the strength of their enemies. They were rushing blindly in, and Ponce, for one, was most displeased.

Not Fiero. A rare grin tugged at the corners of his mouth, as it always did when the time came to spill blood. He stopped behind a small bush, pulled his knife, and pried the bush loose at the roots. Replacing the knife, he held the bush in front of his face and went on.

Every Apache boy had to master the silent stalk. Fiero had been an adept pupil, and among his elders it had long been acknowledged that he was one of the best warriors who had ever worn a Chiricahua breechcloth. His only weakness was his headstrong nature. Too many times he allowed his lust for battle to cloud his judgment.

In this case, as Fiero inched nearer to the bustling camp, as his keen eyes roved among the soldiers and animals, he pondered how he might inflict the most possible damage. There were too many troopers for a frontal attack, and the horses would be so well guarded that stealing a few or running them all off would be next to impossible.

Then Fiero saw the officers, three of them. Long ago he had learned to pick out the leaders by the fancy braids—ribbons and insignia, as the *Nakai-yes* called them—that officers wore. Here were several ripe for the plucking.

The trio sat on a log beside a fire near the trees. Another man was with them. He had a beard and wore a sombrero, and Fiero remembered him as being with the carriage that day on the road to Janos and again at Adobe Wells, trying to prevent the señorita from being taken captive. He must be her father, Fiero guessed. Which meant the soldiers were there to track them down and rescue the woman.

Fiero stopped when one of the younger officers idly gazed toward him. He resumed crawling once no one was looking.

Based on which man wore the most braids and commanded the most attention, Fiero picked the individual in charge. That was the one he decided to kill.

It took over an hour for Fiero to get within 30 feet of the perimeter. He saw bodies of slain soldiers laid out, then covered with blankets, and he wondered who had killed them. Had Clay been there, as Cuchillo Negro suspected?

A long time passed before the camp quieted down. The soldiers fixed their supper and sat up late, talking and drinking coffee. Guards were posted, eight of them spaced at regular intervals. Two more were assigned to safeguard the horses.

Fiero raised his chin from his forearm only after most of the troopers had turned in. The younger officers yawned frequently, but made no move to go to sleep. They appeared content to listen to their commander and the bearded man babble on and on.

Fiero had no such desire. He was not going to lie there all night. Bracing the bush against a clump of grass, he grasped his rifle in both hands, wedged the stock tight to his shoulder, and trained thē barrel on the Mexican with the most insignia. The man was laughing as Fiero touched his finger to the trigger.

Chapter Eleven

The Chiricahuas were not the only ones who heard the din of the aborted battle.

Clay Taggart reined up sharply and twisted in the saddle. He had ridden about a mile south from the campsite with Maria's horse and the pack animal in tow.

The crackle of gunfire puzzled Clay. A good judge of distance, he knew that the gunfire came from the vicinity of the abandoned camp. But he was at a loss to explain it.

The only possibility that made any sense was that the rest of the patrol had arrived on the scene and tangled with Delgadito and company, who must have shown up after he'd left. Yet even that scenario was highly unlikely since Delgadito wasn't fool enough to tangle with a large patrol unless the odds were stacked in his favor, and from the sound of things half the Mexican army was involved.

Clay shrugged and rode on. He was too far away to be of any help even if Delgadito were involved, and he had a pressing matter of his own to deal with, namely recapturing Maria Gonzalez.

He had to hand it to her. She had more grit than he had suspected, and she was almighty clever, to boot. While he had been occupied with the four soldiers, she had fled, but not just in any direction. She had waded into the Rio de Bavisque and hurried off, sticking to the middle of the river, where no one could track her.

Clay had been stumped for a minute, unable to decide which way to go. Maria could have gone north or south. But the latter seemed his best bet since it would take her closer to civilization instead of back toward the Sierra Madre Mountains.

After the shooting died down, Clay clucked his horse into motion and continued searching. Finding Maria in the dark with no tracks to go by was akin to finding the proverbial needle in a haystack, but he was not about to give up. Not because he wanted her as his captive so much as he was concerned for her safety. The wilderness was no place for a green snip of a woman who wouldn't stand a chance if she ran into any of the many beasts, both animal and otherwise, that roamed the vast untamed region.

The notion that he might care enough to be bothered about her welfare disturbed Clay. It went against all his Apache learning to give a hoot for a captive. A warrior was expected to steel his heart to his enemies, and technically Maria was an enemy of the Chiricahuas.

Maybe the problem, Clay reflected, was that he

149

wasn't as much of an Apache as he liked to think. Maybe the values of his white upbringing were too deeply ingrained for him to become just like a full-blooded warrior. Maybe, when all was said and done, he was just kidding himself.

The snap of a twig off to the right brought Clay out of his pensive state. Reining up, he listened, but heard nothing. Nor was there any movement in the brush bordering the river. Maria might be crouched 20 feet away and he would never know it.

In recent months Clay had learned that to survive in the wild a man had to rely on more than logic and common sense. Often intuition played a hand in whether someone lived or died. A man might be approaching a narrow draw and get a bad feeling about the place, or be riding along and have an uneasy feeling that he was being watched by hostile eyes. Those who failed to heed such feelings sometimes paid a fatal price.

Now a feeling came over Clay, not one of impending danger but a conviction that Maria was indeed hidden in that patch of brush and that if he went on by he would never find her. Acting on the impulse, he wheeled his horse and jabbed his heels. The animal snorted as it pounded up the bank and barreled into the vegetation.

Clay rode a score of yards, but flushed nothing. He slowed down and was turning to go back when a slim shape exploded from concealment less than five feet away. Releasing the lead rope, Clay gave chase. He saw her pale face when she glanced back and heard her cry of dismay.

Bending low, Clay pulled alongside of Maria and tried to grab her arm. She veered aside. He narrowed the gap again, but this time when he learned over, he shoved off and tackled her on the fly. They tumbled, winding up with her on top of him.

"I won't let you take me!" Maria said, swinging her small fists. Tears welled in her eyes at the thought of being recaptured after all the trouble she had gone to. She had pushed herself to the point of collapse. All her muscles ached. And in order to travel faster, she had removed her shoes back at the camp. Consequently, her feet were caked with mud and badly cut from the sharp stones on the river bottom and the thorny brush.

Maria had been congratulating herself on her escape when she'd heard a horse splashing down the river. Bolting into the brush, she had squatted, confident the White Apache would be unable to find her. But he had.

Clay Taggart had a frenzied wildcat on his hands. He seized her wrists and heaved to his feet, nearly losing an eye when she lunged, her nails raking his cheek and drawing blood. "Calm down, damn it," he said. "I'm not about to hurt you."

"I won't go! I won't!" Maria said, kicking at his shins.

"You don't have a choice," Clay said. He winced when pain shot up his right leg. "It's for your own good. You wouldn't last two days out here by yourself."

One moment, Maria was struggling and kicking. The next, she collapsed, falling against him, her tears turning into a torrent as all that had happened since her abduction finally took its belated toll. She had tried to be strong for as long as she could. Having her hopes dashed was the last straw.

Clay held her loosely, not quite sure what he should do. Half of him wanted to hold her and assure her that she would be just fine; the other half wanted to slap her around and tell her to quit being such a baby. He did neither. Instead, he waited while she cried herself out.

"You fit to ride now?"

Maria nodded dumbly and permitted him to lead her to his horse. She was thrown into the saddle and the horse was led to the river. There Taggart transferred her to the mount she had been riding before. She heard him urge her to hang on tight, but she didn't care whether she stayed on or not.

Life was too ridiculous for words, Maria decided. What had she done to deserve such misery? How could there be a loving God, as the priests claimed, if people were allowed to suffer so? Did it mean there wasn't a God? Or did it simply mean that God gave men the will to be good or evil as they chose and it had simply been her misfortune to fall into the clutches of the wickedest of all?

Maria was too dazed to think much. She half wished she would die right then and there to spare herself further grief. Life seemed pointless. She would never see her mother and father again, never see their hacienda. So many things she had taken for granted would be denied her forever.

Clay Taggart glanced back when his captive gave a stifled sob. He was going to tell her to be quiet, but suspected his harsh words would make her cry harder.

Bloodbath

The strip of brush along the river was too thick to suit Clay. He was constantly detouring around thickets and briars. Swinging to the west, he entered a line of trees. Far to the north lay Caliente Springs, where he was supposed to rendezvous with the Chiricahuas. He figured he would have to go even farther west in order to avoid whoever had done all the shooting; then he'd circle around to Caliente Springs.

For long minutes they heard nothing but night sounds: The chirp of crickets, the hoot of owls, and the squeak of a bat. All of a sudden, though, the woodland became as silent as a tomb.

Halting, Clay fingered his Winchester. Such profound quiet was unnatural. Predators were near, either animal or human.

The creak and jingle of tack told Clay which. He spotted riders moving along the Rio de Bavisque, five or six of them in all. He could not make out much detail, but he knew they weren't Apaches. The riders were 70 yards away, so there was a very small risk of being discovered.

Clay went on once the men were out of sight, but the woods did not come back to life, as they should have. He was extra vigilant from then on, so he heard the next batch of riders long before he saw them.

There were five, heading south to the west of the trees. Clay saw that they would pass within 15 feet of where he sat, so he moved among a cluster of willows. Maria was slumped over, her long tresses hiding her features. He was glad that she wasn't more alert or she might have yelled to attract them.

Their dusty uniforms stood out against the

backdrop of night. Now Clay had part of the answer, and it was an answer he didn't like. How many more groups of soldiers were in the area? And who were they after?

The second bunch had gone by and Clay was raising his reins to go on when that which he had suspected would happen did. Maria had seen the troopers and raised her voice loud enough to be heard clear down in Mexico City.

"Soldiers! Soldiers! Help me! The White Apache has taken me captive!"

Cursing, Clay fled, hauling hard on the lead rope. Coarse shouts confirmed the soldiers were in pursuit. Clay skirted a log and dashed between two willows. To the rear a carbine blasted and the slug bit into the willow on the left.

Clay was in a tight spot. Outrunning the soldiers was a hopeless proposition, what with him being slowed down by the other two horses. Nor would it be smart to make a stand. In addition to being outnumbered, he never knew when Maria might turn on him to keep him distracted so the troopers could finish him off.

Another complication reared its ugly head when from the northeast a man shouted in Spanish, "This is Maj. Filisola! We are on our way, Sergeant!"

Soldiers were all over the place. Clay cut to the northwest, pushing the horses as best he could. The crack of branches and the thud of hooves warned him the first bunch of soldiers were getting too close for comfort.

Shifting, Clay banged a shot at a vague target and was rewarded by a yelp of agony and the crash of a body hitting the ground.

Bloodbath

Striking northward again, Clay sought to out-distance the rest, but it was as he had thought it would be: they gained rapidly. And all the time, bearing down on him from the northeast, came the major and more troopers. He had to trust in luck and pray the soldiers would lose interest if he could give them the slip.

Unknown to Clay Taggart, Maj. Vicente Filisola was not about to ever lose interest. Not only was he anxious to save the senorita of his dreams; he was eager to avenge the death of a man he had looked up to as the best military mind in the Mexican Army.

Col. Jose Gonzalez had been shot smack between the eyes by an Apache lurking in the dark. He had died instantly, his mouth slack, his tongue lolling. The colonel had resembled a poled ox more than a distinguished commander.

The camp had been in an uproar. Enraged troopers had rushed every which way, seeking targets that weren't there. Filisola and Mora had rallied the panicked men and organized a thorough search of the immediate vicinity, but found no trace of the shooter.

There had been that one shot, no more. The two majors agreed that it had to have been the work of Apaches, who had melted into the night as silently as they had come.

But Filisola was not to be so easily thwarted. As senior officer, he had ordered a sweep of the area for miles around, with the goal of flushing the Apaches into the open. Deep down, he'd doubted it would produce results. Then, to his fierce delight, he had heard the sweet voice of the colonel's niece. Nothing short of death would stop

155

him from saving her. In the bargain he would put an end to the depredations of the White Apache.

Clay Taggart had no idea he was up against four dozen vengeful soldiers spread out over a five miles radius. To him they were ordinary troopers, and ordinary troopers more often than not would run from Apaches rather than tangle with them.

From the sound of things, Clay knew the two groups would soon be on him. He had to act and act fast or he would never get revenge on Miles Gillett. He would die there by the Rio de Bavisque, unmourned, his body left to rot.

It would be a cold day in hell before Clay let that happen. Plunging into thick timber, he drew rein and jumped down. Maria attempted to resist when he grasped her wrist and pulled, but she was too weak and weary to keep from falling next to him. Streaking out his Bowie, he cut the lead rope to both her horse and the packhorse.

"What are you—" Maria said.

"Quiet," Clay said and rapped her lightly on the skull with the hilt of his knife. She slumped, dazed but not unconscious. Quickly Clay seized the bridle to her animal and swung it around so that it faced due south. Then he positioned the packhorse, facing it due north. The animals stood tail to tail.

Sheathing the Bowie, Clay stepped between the horses. He gave her mount a resounding smack on the rump, pivoted, and did the same to the pack animals. They promptly snorted and sped off, making as much noise as a herd of buffalo.

Clay crouched beside Maria and gripped the reins to his horse so it wouldn't get it into its head to join the others. He watched the other

Bloodbath

animals break from the timber and listened to yells from the soldiers and the boom of guns.

Would they take the bait? That was the crucial question. Clay observed horsemen racing in both directions and heard someone shout orders.

Clay stayed put until the hoofbeats faded. His ruse had bought some time, but not much. It wouldn't be long before the soldiers caught the riderless horses and realized they had been duped.

Hooking an arm around Maria's slim waist, Clay slung her onto the saddle as if flinging a sack of grain. He held her up with one hand while mounting in back of her. Then he turned to the west and departed.

So far, so good, Clay thought. Maj. Filisola and his men were being led on a wild-goose chase. If he could reach the foothills, he'd lose them. He selected grassy tracts that muffled his animal's tread and shied from open spaces.

More shouting filled the air, from the southeast this time. More troopers were coming. Clay angled to the southwest. He rode half a mile without encountering another soldier. Evidently his quick thinking had bailed his hide out of the fire.

Presently Clay looped toward the northwest. His original destination was the same. Delgadito would be waiting for him at Caliente Springs.

Three shots broke the silence. Clay surmised it was a signal but he had no inkling for what. Coming on mesquite, he prodded his horse into a trot. Maria swayed, still woozy, her shoulders bumping his chest. He thought that he heard her mutter a few words.

By all rights Clay should have been a bundle of nerves. Clay Taggart, the rancher, would have been. But Clay Taggart, the White Apache, found himself thrilling to the challenge of outwitting a company of soldiers. He exercised caution as an Apache would, relying on the skills he had honed under Delgadito's tutelage.

Some minutes passed before the wind brought him the sounds of three more pistol shots, the same signal as before, only farther away.

Taggart barely slowed down. He was positive he had given the soldiers the slip. By his reckoning he was well to the northwest of the river and could slant to a more northerly heading anytime he wanted.

"Please let me go."

The soft appeal caught Clay off guard. "I thought you were out to the world."

"Please," Maria said. "This is my last chance. You are my only hope."

"Then you don't have any hope," Clay said testily and regretted being needlessly cruel.

"What manner of man are you? You have turned your back on everything you knew and sided with the bitter enemies of your people. You have killed many innocents. And now you would send my soul to a living hell. Why? What have I ever done to you?"

"You ask too damn many questions."

Maria felt more tears fill her eyes and blinked them away. The time for tears was past. She must use her wits as she had never used them before. Appealing to his greed had not worked because he was one of those rare men who did not value money. But perhaps appealing to his conscience would have the desired effect. Buried somewhere under that hard exterior must be a shred of compassion. There had to be!

"You told me that you loved a woman once."

"I don't care to talk about her," Clay snapped. The reminder seared a red-hot branding iron of remorse into his gut.

"It's not her I want to talk about. It's love," Maria said. "Any man who can love another can't be all bad. You must have some decency left inside of you. I'm appealing to that decency. I'm begging you to let me go before we rejoin the Apaches."

"I can't."

Maria turned, her face inches from his. "Why must you be so stubborn? Why do you always let your pride stand in the way of doing that which you know to be right?"

"Be quiet."

"I will not," Maria said, defying him. "Not when all I hold dear is at stake. Didn't you have a mother and a father? How can you tear me away from mine? My mother will go crazy with grief. My father will wither away little by little. And all because you are playing at being an Apache."

Clay resisted an urge to smack her. "I'm not playing. The Apaches are my pards."

"Maybe so, but the truth is that they are Apaches and you are not. No matter how long you live among them, no matter how many of their ways you adopt as your own, deep inside you will always be white."

"That's where you're wrong. Being an Apache is more than dressing as they do and living as they do. I could never expect you to understand

159

because I reckon I don't know quite how to put it into words. It has to do with thinking like them, with knowing that you're at the bottom of the barrel and have nowhere to go but up."

"And that gives you the right to go around killing people as you see fit, senor? That gives you the right to kidnap women who have never done you any harm?"

Clay cocked his head to listen. It was a grave mistake to let her divert his attention when there might be soldiers within earshot but he could not bring himself to clip her on the jaw.

"Can't you answer me because you know that you are in the wrong?"

"Who's to say what's right and what's wrong anymore?" Clay said. "I figured that I knew once, and then my whole world was turned inside out. My woman turned on me. My friends turned on me. Even my government turned on me. And it taught me a valuable lesson."

"Which is?"

"That when a man has nothing to lose, he'll try anything. That it's every hombre for himself, and the devil take the hindmost."

"You can't really believe that?"

"I believe this," Clay said and patted his rifle. "I believe in the law of the gun. I believe in the old saying about an eye for an eye, a tooth for a tooth. I believe that making those who have wronged you pay is better than turning the other cheek like a Bible thumper."

"If that is true, then I pity you."

"Save your pity for yourself."

Maria faced around. "You have lost your soul to the devil, Clay Taggart. I would not want to be in your shoes when you are called to account."

The wind picked up, knifing down off the Sierra Madres to rustle the mesquite and stir Clay's long hair. He shut her words from his mind, refusing to give them any consideration. Maybe she was right, maybe she wasn't. But he had picked the trail he aimed to follow and he intended to play his hand out, come what may. No matter what else was said about the White Apache, no one would ever be able to accuse him of being a coward.

Clay reined the horse to the north, guided by the North Star. He would reach Caliente Springs by noon if he didn't run into more patrols. From there it would be a clear shot to the border and safety. He rose in the stirrups once more to make a final survey of the country behind him. Satisfied he had outstripped any pursuit, he goaded the horse to a gallop, never knowing that he was wrong.

Mere seconds after the sound of the White Apache's mount faded on the breeze, a bulky silhouette detached itself from the mesquite. It was Pedro the tracker, who had gone off by his own to find the Apaches who killed the brother of his boss. He had wanted to hunt alone rather than be burdened with noisy soldiers who didn't know the first thing about stalking at night. And it had paid off.

Pedro stared after the renegade a few moments, then wheeled his horse and rode hell for leather toward the camp. He knew where the White Apache was going, and he smiled to himself as he rode.

"We have you now, butcher."

161

Chapter Twelve

The desert was an inferno. A golden cauldron dominated the sky, scorching all life below. Plants drooped, withered by the heat. Animals were sheltered in their burrows or wherever they could find tiny patches of shade.

Across the parched landscape plodded the White Apache's stolen mount. In the saddle sagged Maria Gonzalez, her face baked red, her chin touching her chest. She would have fallen off long ago had the White Apache not lashed her wrists to the saddle horn and her ankles to the stirrups.

Clay himself walked, leading the animal by the reins. The blistering oven, which once would have melted him as a flame melted a candle, hardly fazed him at all. Where once he would have been caked with sweat from head to toe, the only concession his body made to the scalding temperature were a few beads of perspiration on his brow below his headband.

Caliente Springs lay less than half an hour away. Clay had pushed the horse to get there because he didn't care to be left behind by the rest of the band. Whether the animal lived or died was of no consequence to him; he'd butcher the carcass, eat what he could, and dry some of the flesh for later use, just as any Chiricahua warrior would.

For over an hour Clay had tramped on, looking neither right nor left, his mind in a turmoil that his face didn't show. As would any full-blooded warrior, he was becoming more and more adept at hiding his feelings, at keeping his features as impassive as stone so that his true emotions were known only to himself.

He was in conflict with himself. His white upbringing raged fiery war with the Apache ways he had adopted, and neither was able to gain the upper hand. The internal war boiled down to one burning issue. What was he to do with Maria Gonzalez? The white part of him wanted to let her go so she could be reunited with her family. The Apache part of him wanted to keep her as his wife, maybe the first of several he would take, provided he let her live along enough.

For two bits he would have been tempted to throttle her senseless. Her words of the night before had started the conflict, and no matter how he tried, he couldn't put it from his mind. Was he as she claimed, white? Or was he, as he believed, more like an Apache? Or did the truth lie somewhere in between?

Clay had wrestled with the problem for so long that he was tired of thinking. He absently stretched and swept the horizon on all sides, a precaution every Chiricahua learned to make as much of a habit as breathing.

A spiraling cloud of dust highlighted the southern horizon.

Clay's jaw muscles twitched. He had been careless. He had been deep in thought when he should have been keeping his eyes peeled.

The size of the cloud indicated a large party on horseback. It had be soldiers, either the same bunch he had tangled with at the river or a different one. They were riding hard, from the look of things, unusual for troopers in broad daylight—unless they were after someone.

Breaking into a trot, Clay yanked on the reins to get the horse to keep pace. Maria snapped awake and looked sluggishly around, then sagged again, too fatigued to care about anything other than the rest she craved.

For 15 minutes Clay rode northward. At last a ragged ridge appeared. Caliente Springs was located in a narrow gap near the summit. The springs were so remote that few Mexican or white travelers ever visited them although they were used regularly by Indians.

Clay had visited the site several times. On the other side of the ridge stretched miles of chaparral laced by thorny thickets. Once there, the band would elude the soldier with ease.

The brown ridge grew in size. A threadbare path meandered up toward the gap, curving among a field littered with boulders of every size, shape, and description. The gap was shrouded in shadow.

At the edge of the boulder field, Clay stopped.

Swiftly, he cut Maria free and lowered her to the ground. She came back to life and glared at him.

"What are you up to now, Senor Taggart?

He knew why she called him by his given name rather than the one bestowed on him by Delgadito, but he refused to be taken in by her tricks, refused to see himself as more white than otherwise. He also refused to answer. Gripping her wrist, he walked her between a pair of towering boulders spaced barely wide enough apart for a rider to pass through. "Don't move," he said.

Clay coaxed the horse into the space. One arm draped around the animal's neck to reassure it, he suddenly lanced the Bowie into the animal's throat and wrenched mightily. Flesh sheared, blood spurted. The horse tried to buck but was too exhausted.

Gradually the mount weakened. The ground was soaked a bright red when Clay let go and rejoined Maria.

Snorting and swaying, the horse tried to back into the open but its front legs buckled. It sank down right there, blocking the trail. Blood caked its chest and forelegs.

"How could you?" Maria asked. "That was a sadistic thing to do. There was no reason to hurt the poor creature."

"Oh?" Clay pointed at the dust cloud, now much closer and much larger.

Marie was all too aware what the cloud meant and became deliriously excited by the idea she might soon be rescued. She figured out that Taggart had killed the horse to block the trail and give them more time to reach the top. The devil didn't miss a trick, she mused.

Clay was about to leave when he remembered the Henry. Stepping around the spreading pool of blood, he plucked it from the saddle boot. Then, with a rifle in either hand, he nudged the woman and they started to ascend.

High above them four pair of dark eagle eyes watched with interest.

"He will not make it in time," Delgadito said.

"He will if he lets go of the woman," Fiero said. "I would, were I in his moccasins."

Out on the flatland, six dust-choked riders galloped toward the ridge in advance of the main body of troopers and vaqueros. Among them rode Maj. Vicente Filisola, who should have ridden with the main column as would any other commanding officer. But he was too upset about Maria, too worried the Apaches would spirit her away. So with Pedro, Sgt. Amat, and three of his best riders, he had gone on ahead of the column to see if he could slow Maria's abductor down.

The tracker was the first to spy a patch of light blue on the ridge. "Captain! That is the color of the dress the senorita wore."

Filisola looked and his blood raced like lightning. "Faster, men!" he said. "We must not let that devil get over the ridge or we will never see her again!"

Clay saw the six riders sweeping toward him. In the distance was a growing knot of soldiers. He was hopelessly outnumbered, but not about to give up without a fight.

Apaches were more than a match for their longstanding rivals. Normally soldiers fled rather than fought. But this time the honor and life of a young woman was at stake. And it has been forever true that in the breast of the most callous of men often beats a soft heart for a fair maiden in distress.

So the soldiers arrived on the scene bent on vengeance for the beloved commanding officer they had lost and determined to save his precious niece at all costs.

Clay climbed as rapidly as his captive's condition allowed. She stumbled so often that he suspected she was trying to slow him down and hauled on her arm so hard it nearly popped out of the socket. "No tricks," he growled.

Maj. Filisola came to the beginning of the trail and fumed when he saw the dead horse blocking the way. Vaulting to the ground, he waved his saber. "Upward, men! Before she is lost to us!"

Getting a running start, Filisola flew toward the dead horse and sailed over it in a single leap. He went on without looking back. Let the others come as they may, he reflected. He was going to rescue Maria.

The major saw a flash of blue above him. Tilting his head back, he spotted Maria and her captor. An icy chill rippled down his spine at the mental picture of the violation that would occur if he failed her. "I'm coming, Senorita! Have hope!"

Maria Gonzalez heard and remembered the dashing young officer. She dug in her heels. "Let me go! Please!"

Clay turned a deaf ear to her plea. Jerking her arm violently, he climbed higher. A rifle cracked below them and a slug ricocheted off a boulder to their left.

Below, Maj. Filisola spun and frowned at the smoking rifle in Pedro's hands. "Are you loco? You might hit her by mistake."

"We must slow him down until the rest get here," the tracker replied. "You know as well as I do that, if he gets over the ridge, all is lost."

Clay came to an open grade. On either hand were jumbled boulders, a treacherous maze the woman was incapable of negotiating. He had no choice but to go straight up. "Move quickly if you value your life," he said, giving her a shove. They went only a few feet, however, when the air rang with gunfire. Bullets smacked into the earth all around them. He felt a stinging sensation in his calf, another on his shoulder.

Throwing Maria behind a boulder, Clay brought his Winchester to bear. His first shot toppled a soldier and drove the rest to cover. They replied with a barrage of lead that kept him pinned down.

And all the while, the main body of soldiers galloped nearer and nearer.

Clay was fit to be tied. He was close to the summit, but it might as well be on the moon. He could readily escape, but not dragging a woman along. Still, he refused to leave her.

Filisola and his small group of avengers slowly worked upward. Glancing back, he saw Martin Gonzalez and Maj. Mora. In another few moments the ridge would be swarming with dozens of soldiers. The White Apache's days of pillaging and plundering were almost over.

The object of the major's bloodlust realized the same fact. Clay looked down at the woman at his feet, and she met his gaze defiantly. She was no longer the timid girl he had snatched at

Bloodbath

Adobe Wells. The crucible of hardship had forged a miraculous change.

"Leave me," Maria said. Her flagging spirit had been revitalized by the appearance of the soldiers. Instinctively she knew they were her last, best hope of escaping. Her moment of truth had arrived, and she was ready.

"Never," Clay said and leaned against the boulder to feed cartridges into his rifle. He didn't hear her move, but he abruptly sensed that she had, and pivoting, he was just in time to ward off a brutal blow that would have caved in his skull had it landed.

Maria stepped back, the big rock she clutched poised to strike again. "I'll die before I'll let you take me!"

"That's what you think," Clay said. Feinting a step to the right, he suckered her into swinging, and as the rock cleaved the air, he delivered a solid hit to her stomach with the butt of his rifle. She collapsed, breathing heavily. The rock fell from her limp fingers.

"Damn you! Damn you all to hell, White Apache!"

Another volley blasted below. This one was twice as loud and lasted twice as long. Leaden hornets buzzed overhead and spanged off the boulders.

The rest of the soldiers had arrived and were fanning out, firing as they ran. Clay saw the same bearded man in a sombrero whom he had seen at Abobe Wells. It was her father, he figured, and fixed a bead on the man's sternum. He had the man dead to rights. All he had to do was squeeze the trigger.

169

"If I had your knife, I would kill you!" Maria spat.

Clay smiled and fired.

Down the slope, Martin Gonzalez's sombrero went flying and he dived for cover.

"I would peel your skin from you like Apaches do to our people," Maria said spitefully. "I would rip out your tongue and feed it to the buzzards."

"I believe you would," Clay said. A pair of troopers drew his fire and both went down, sporting new nostrils. "You are my kind of woman, sweet thing."

"How dare you!" Maria cried, punching his leg. "It is true what they say. You are a monster!"

"I try."

So many soldiers dotted the ridge that crossing the open grade invited certain death. Clay grabbed her wrist and tried anyway, dragging her after him. Farther down someone shouted and the shots tapered off.

Then someone else yelled, "Don't let him take my baby!"

Smoke and slugs filled the air. To Clay, it was as if he stood in the middle of a rain of bullets that chipped the rocks at his feet and crisscrossed the air around him. How they all missed, he would never know.

Lunging to the sanctuary of the boulder, Clay pushed Maria down and crouched to take stock of the situation. The shooting tapered off, but didn't stop. He could see the summit and the gap 40 yards above him, but reaching it was impossible unless he could turn invisible to cross the grade— or if he had a shield.

Inspiration prompted Clay to pounce on Maria

and seize her from behind. Hooking his left arm around her waist, he said in her ear, "Now we'll see how much your father really loves you."

"What are you—" Maria began, bewildered. Terror gnawed at her vitals but she suppressed it. She knew that now was not the time to give in to her fear or she wouldn't live long enough to see the next dawn.

Clay sidled into the open, holding Maria in front of him, facing his enemies. He contrived to contort himself so that the only target the soldiers and vaqueros had was his captive. Backing slowly, he began to climb the grade again.

Maj. Filisola tingled with horror at the sight of the lovely woman he had come to adore being used so callously. He heard carbines being worked and men rising to shoot. "Hold your fire!" he roared. "Anyone who pulls a trigger faces a firing squad! So help me!"

Nearby, Martin Gonzalez paused with his rifle leveled. "She is my daughter, Major," he called out. "I have the final say, and I say that we must not let him get away with her. Under no circumstances. Do you understand?"

"No one fire!" Filisola repeated.

"Didn't you hear me?" Martin said. "Even if it means her life, we can't let her fall into Apache hands."

"Your brother felt the same," Filisola said. "I did not agree with him, and I do not agree with you."

For moments that seemed like an eternity, there was a stalemate. Clay continued to back upward, Maria frozen in his grasp, while the soldiers and vaqueros watched, uncertain what to do. Many had risen in their eagerness to shoot. Filisola held his breath, willing Maria and the renegade to reach safety swiftly, aware a nervous twitch would result in a bloodbath.

It was at this instant that another element entered the fray. Delgadito, Cuchillo Negro, Fiero, and Ponce had descended to the top of the grade without being seen. Cuchillo Negro had started down first and the rest had followed. Now, as one, they showed themselves, fired several shots apiece, and ducked down again.

Caught completely off guard, the soldiers and vaqueros lost six of their number and half again as many were wounded before the others got over their shock and cut loose with reckless ferocity. Carbines, rifles, and pistols blended in a lethal litany that rivaled the crash of thunder.

"No!" Maj. Filisola said. "For God's sake, stop!"

But no one listened, not even the few who heard him over the din. Their mortal enemies were above them. There wasn't a man present who hadn't lost a relative or a friend to Apaches. They fired and fired and fired, then reloaded when their guns went empty. Many charged.

Caught in the middle were Clay and Maria Gonzalez. Slugs peppered the area around them, zinged off rocks, nicked their bodies. He went faster but the lead followed them as if drawn by a magnet.

Maria was panic-stricken. She didn't want to be. She wanted to be brave and to hold her chin high. But the knowledge that she was a heartbeat from death shattered her newfound courage and left her cringing in fear. She made a tremendous effort to marshal her courage. Then she was struck.

Clay heard her cry, felt her buckle, and saw the red splotch on her left thigh. They were almost to the top of the grade. A few more steps, and her father would never set eyes on her again. The Apaches were shooting steadily, trying to stop the onrushing Mexicans, but there were too many.

Suddenly Clay reached the top. Bullets were as thick as hail. They chewed into the ground and bit into boulders. A short jump would carry them out of reach, and he girded his legs.

Maria's agony had dispelled her fear. She twisted, realized she was yards away from certain captivity, and threw herself forward, attempting to unbalance her captor.

The trick nearly worked. Clay dug his soles into the soil and clung to her, his biceps rippling. He fell to one knee for added purchase.

Fighting like a wildcat, Maria tried to break free. She screamed when he pulled her higher despite her frantic struggling.

Clay surged upward, hauling her over the rim. Maria tried to turn and scratch his eyes out. He gave her a cuff that brought blood to her lips, then locked her arm in a vise of iron and hastened upward.

When Maj. Filisola saw Maria vanish, his mind went blank with dread. He forgot his military training, forgot every rule he had ever learned about engaging Apaches in combat. Raising his saber on high, he sprinted up the ridge. "After them, men! Save the senorita!"

The Chiricahuas had held out as long as they

dared. With soldiers coming at them from several directions, they had to get out of there. Delgadito melted into the boulders and was immediately joined by Fiero and Ponce. Cuchillo Negro delayed long enough to drop a vaquero; then he too made for the summit with the speed and agility of a mountain sheep.

To steal without being caught. To kill without being killed. Those were the Apache creeds. None of the warriors, including Cuchillo Negro, were willing to sacrifice themselves needlessly. They had done what they could to help Lickoyee-shisinday. Whether he made it to the summit was entirely up to him.

Clay wasn't far behind them. Maria had gone limp with shock and offered no resistance. Slugs zipped by now and then but none came close enough to pose a threat. He knew he had won, knew she was as good as his, and his smile returned.

The last stretch appeared, a tunnel of sorts formed by massive slabs that had toppled and leaned against one another. Clay ran through to the sunlight beyond. A few more strides brought him to the gap. He was ten feet below the summit. The Chiricahuas were already halfway to the other side. Cuchillo Negro beckoned him to hurry.

Troopers and vaqueros choked the trail. In the forefront was a young officer brandishing a saber, the look of a madman on his face.

Clay faced Maria. Tears ran down her cheeks and her shoulders shook in convulsive sobs.

"I hate you! I'll hate you forever!" she said.

The White Apache knew differently. She would

Bloodbath

be just like other women taken by the Apaches. At first she would be moody and refuse to do as she was told. In time, though, she would realize her plight was hopeless and accept her fate and settle into the routine of Apache life. Much later, she might even come to enjoy living again.

Clay glanced at the warriors, then at the Mexicans. He reached out and caressed Maria's chin. "You are mine, woman—if I wanted you."

So saying, he kicked her in the stomach, knocking her off her feet and sending her tumbling down the slope. He lingered long enough to see the shocked amazement on her face when she sat up. Then he spun and ran.

The warriors were waiting. For once their emotions showed. Each wore a quizzical expression, and it was Cuchillo Negro who voiced the question uppermost on all their minds. "Why?"

"She was too weak to make a fitting wife," Clay said. Taking charge, he led them toward the chaparral, where they would disappear as if the earth had swallowed them, while over the crown of the ridge came cries of joy.